ACTIONS SPEAK LOUDER

Now that Bolt had the one woman he wanted in his room, he was at a loss for what to offer her. "You want whiskey?" he asked. "It's all I got."

"Not really, thanks." When she smiled, small indentations dimpled her cheeks.

"Well, I'll be damned. You got dimples! I heard tell that women with dimples have . . ."

"Yes," she coaxed. "Have what?"

"Never mind," he responded with a half-smile.

"Now you've got me curious!" she persisted, melting Bolt with her hot sultry stare. Then she came to him, like some starved animal, sliding her arms over his shoulders. He drew her tight and lifted her head to kiss her mouth. Her lips were warm, moist. She pressed her tall slender body against him as he brought his hand up and began unbuttoning her dress. The buttons went all the way down to the hem, but Bolt didn't bother with them all—just enough to finish where his sentence left off. . . .

THE DYNAMIC NEW WARHUNTER SERIES

THE WARHUNTER #1: KILLER'S COUNCIL   (729-5, $1.95)
by Scott Siegel
Warfield Hunter and the Farrel gang shoot out their bloody feud
in the little town of Kimble, where War Hunter saves the sheriff's
life. Soon enough, he learns it was a set-up—and he has to take on
a whole town singlehandedly!

THE WARHUNTER #2: GUNMEN'S GRAVEYARD

                                        (743-0, $1.95)
by Scott Siegel
When War Hunter escapes from the Comanches, he's stuck with
a souvenir—a poisoned arrow in his side. The parched, feverish
man lying in the dust is grateful when he sees two men riding his
way—until he discovers he's at the mercy of the same bandits who
once robbed him and left him for dead!

THE WARHUNTER #3:
THE GREAT SALT LAKE MASSACRE   (785-6, $2.25)
by Scott Siegel
War Hunter knew he was asking for trouble when he let lovely
Ella Phillips travel with him. It wasn't long in coming, and when
Hunter took off, there was one corpse behind him. Little did he
know he was headed straight for a rampaging band of hotheaded
Utes!

*Available wherever paperbacks are sold, or order direct from the
Publisher. Send cover price plus 50¢ per copy for mailing and
handling to Zebra Books, 475 Park Avenue South, New York,
N.Y. 10016. DO NOT SEND CASH.*

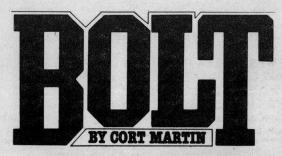

BOLT

BY CORT MARTIN

SHOWDOWN AT BLACK MESA

#3

ZEBRA BOOKS
KENSINGTON PUBLISHING CORP.

ZEBRA BOOKS

are published by

KENSINGTON PUBLISHING CORP.
475 Park Avenue South
New York, N.Y. 10016

Printed in the United States of America

CHAPTER ONE

Bolt felt the tension the minute he stepped inside the Pawnee Saloon.

A hush fell over the room as the batwing doors swung shut behind him and his friend, Tom Penrod. Their boots crunching on the sawdust-littered floor was the only sound they heard as the gawkers held their breath in unison.

It was a silence born of curiosity.

Bolt had felt the silence before. In other saloons. In other towns off the beaten trail.

A dozen pairs of eyes followed the two strangers as they made their way through the half-empty tables to the long bar to the right of the entrance. Other men, clustered at the bar, glared at the two tall strangers, shifting slightly to make room for them.

Bolt stared back at them with cold blue eyes until the men turned their heads away.

"What is this?" asked Bolt, "some kind of wake?"

"Yair," said Tom, "did someone die in here?"

No one answered them.

The Pawnee Saloon smelled of beer and cigar smoke, sweat and horse manure. Coal oil lanterns hung at regular intervals throughout the room, with one adorning each end of the long mirror behind the bar. Advertisements for Zang's beer were prominently displayed to entice those who came to slake their thirsts. A mural of half-nude women bathing at a river tilted at a slight angle above the mirror.

"Is it always this quiet?" Bolt asked when the bartender came to take their orders.

"Not always."

Bolt detected the sarcasm in the bartender's voice.

Once Bolt and Penrod settled themselves on high barstools, the bustle of business took up where it had left off. The tinkle of glasses. The uneasy shifting of bodies as the men at the tables made themselves comfortable again. The *swick-swick* of cards as the men at the back table resumed their poker game. The loud voices of drunken men.

All the sounds Bolt had heard before. At a hundred other saloons in the west.

The bartender, Lenny Haskins, was a tall, gaunt man with a sallow complexion and a shiny head that was balding before its time. The towel flung over his shoulder was stained gray and grimy, reeked of tanglefoot and stale beer. The long white apron he wore below his vest was equally damp and mottled.

"Whiskies. Two of 'em." Bolt flexed his broad shoulders, loosening saddle-sore muscles. He was whip-lean, muscular. His shoulder length coal black hair was beginning to look shabby. He ran a hand over the stubble growing on his strong square jaw.

"I could use a bath and a shave."

"You sure could," grinned Tom Penrod. "Me too."

6

Tom was slightly shorter than his friend, thinner. His gangly look made him seem younger than Bolt. But they were the same age. Twenty-four. The natural curl in his dark brown hair always gave him the look of a tousle-headed youngster. His eyes were hazel, but sometimes when they took on the color of his surroundings, they seemed as blue as Bolt's eyes.

Bolt heard the whispering behind him. He couldn't make out what the two men were saying. The Mexican and the dark-haired jasper with the beady eyes. But he knew it concerned him. Tom, too, probably.

Bolt studied the images in the mirror behind the bar, saw the two men huddled together, exchanging words. He watched as they lowered their heads in secrecy, then lifted their eyes to stare at his back.

"Something's wrong," Bolt said quietly without turning around.

"Think so?" Tom asked.

"Yeah. Those two sittin' behind us got us tagged. Think those wanted posters on us got this far?"

"Could be."

Bolt hoped there wouldn't be any trouble. He didn't need it now. Not after five days in the saddle. He wouldn't even be in this God-forsaken town if an old friend of his wasn't in trouble.

Black Mesa. A town somewhere in west Oklahoma, in the panhandle. A bad town. A town where no town should be. Outlaw-ridden, off the beaten trail. A rich town, nonetheless. Rich because of good land and the proximity of the Cimarron River.

"That's him all right," whispered Jack Batson, one of the men who sat at a table behind Bolt.

"You sure?" said Joe Chato, glancing up at the stranger at the bar through bleary eyes.

"Damn right I'm sure. I saw the poster. I oughta know."

"I didn't see no poster."

"Over to the jail. The other night when the sheriff locked me up fer bein' drunk. They was a poster of that outlaw. Had his picture on it. His name's Bolt. Odd name, ain't it?"

"What's he wanted for?"

"Murder. Bank robbery. Probably other things. He had a partner in the bank heist. Name of Penrose or Penrod. Somethin' like that. That's probably the feller sittin' next to him. We can pick up some easy reward money."

"How much?"

"Two thousand big ones!"

"Chit!"

They were just drunk enough to try it.

The bartender got the drift of their conversation when he delivered fresh whiskey and beer chasers to their table. He didn't like what he heard. These two men were double-fisted drinkers, but they couldn't handle their booze. They had already caused Lenny too many headaches with their drunken antics. If they started anything today, he'd kick them out on their ass, never let them inside the Pawnee again.

Haskins wiped spilled beer from the table with his stained towel, held the painted tray out until Jack Batson dug deep in his pocket for the coins to pay for the last round of drinks. He shook his head in disgust as he walked back to the bar.

"You call him out, Chato," Batson whispered

8

when the bartender was gone. "I'll have my pistol out under the table."

"*Si*, let's keel heem. The ugly peeg. Get us some spendin' money."

Lenny Haskins shuffled back behind the bar, leaned over between Bolt and Penrod and spoke in a low voice.

"Be a good idear if you fellers drink up and move on."

Bolt shot him a hard look.

"You kickin' us out?"

"I'm askin'," said Haskins. "There's gonna be trouble if you stay."

"That's a shame," Bolt said sarcastically. "We're just gettin' settled in. We're ready for another drink, ain't we, Tom?"

"Yair. Like my friend says, we plan to stay a while."

"Make it two more of the same, barkeep," said Bolt.

"I'm warning you. Them two cowhands is getting mean drunk. They got themselves a bad reputation when they get too much booze in their bellies. That's when they get in a fighting mood."

"I'll keep that in mind," Bolt said.

"I'm tellin' ya, there's gonna be bloodshed if you stay. They've singled you out. They're saying you're an outlaw and that you got a fat price on your head."

"Drunk thinking. Don't worry about it. Just bring us another drink."

Bolt glanced up at the mirror. He couldn't see the reflection of the two troublemakers. The bartender was blocking his view.

"I don't want no trouble in here, that's all," Haskins mumbled as he reached for the bottle to refill their smudgy glasses.

Penrod rolled a cigarette, lit it with a sulphur match. The smoke curled up between him and the bartender.

"Where can we find some women around here?" Tom asked.

"The purtiest gals can be found at the Panhandle Club," said Haskins. "Kinda early for them, though. They work at night, you know. Only one place in town has day time gals. The Roosters Nest." Lenny swiped a cloth across the counter, nervously watched the drunks at the table. He saw Jack Batson check his pistol, leer at Bolt's back. Lenny moved slowly away from Bolt, polishing the bar top as he went.

"Panhandle Club," said Bolt. "That where Belinda works?" He was talking to Tom, but his attention was focused on the reflection of the Mexican and the dark-eyed man.

A puff of smoke from Tom's cigarette clouded the image briefly. Bolt waited until it drifted away, then watched as the Mexican grinned and glanced in his direction. White teeth against dark skin. The other man had a mean look in his beady eyes, a sneer on his lips.

"Yair," said Tom, "that's the place she mentioned."

"She a glitter gal?"

"Said she was a singer. A dancer. I don't reckon she gets paid for anything else."

Bolt watched the reflection in the dusty mirror. He saw the man with the rumpled shirt and beady eyes

10

slide a pistol from its holster, conceal it under the table. Bolt leaned close to Tom, spoke in a soft voice.

"Take out the Mex if there's trouble. I'll handle the other one."

Tom nodded his head.

Lenny Haskins saw it coming. He walked to the other end of the bar, as far away from Bolt and Penrod as he could get.

"Hey, ugly one," taunted Chato. "You make me a leetle seek."

"You talkin' to me, Mex?" Bolt turned slowly, eased off the bar stool, his cold blue eyes boring into the Mexican's. His right hand hung loose.

The men at the bar stopped drinking, turned to watch the confrontation between the strangers and the troublemakers. They slid off their stools, began moving away, giving Bolt a wide berth.

Bolt made a quick scan of their faces, wondered if any of them were in cahoots with the goading Mex and his friend.

Chairs screeched across the wooden floor as men at other tables got up, fanned out in a big circle. Some of them found a safe place near the far wall. A few of them inched toward the batwing doors.

The poker game came to a halt. Every eye in the saloon was on the four men near the middle of the room.

"Yeah, *gringo*. You look like a peeg."

"Likely you've had too much Zang's or mixed too many parts whiskey with it."

On the outside, Bolt appeared calm. Inside he seethed. Muscles rippled with tautness. His breathing became deeper, more measured. A knot formed at the back of his neck. His right hand hovered over his pistol. He knew that Batson's pistol was already out of its holster, hidden beneath the table.

"I don't like road tramps," heckled Chato. "This is a private town."

"Make your own room, Mex."

Chato went for his pistol.

Tom was ready. His hand darted to his holster. He fired at the Mexican just as his pistol cleared leather, cocked and aimed.

Chato was a second too late drawing his pistol. He squeezed the trigger just as Tom's bullet pierced his heart. The wild shot shattered a bottle on a shelf behind the bar, spanged through the mirror behind it. The exploding bottle sent other bottles flying from the shelf, crashing to the floor. Splintered glass flew in all directions.

Before Jack Batson could raise his pistol high enough to shoot, Bolt shot from the hip. The bullet drilled through Batson's forehead, right between his beady eyes.

Batson's mouth fell open in surprise as his head snapped backwards from the impact. He took a step forward, trying to regain his balance. His body went limp and toppled forward.

He was dead before his face smacked into the hard floor. The back of his head blown apart. Blood and gray brain matter splattered in all directions, clinging to the table leg, the chair legs, soaking into the sawdust on the floor.

Bolt stepped back against the bar. He looked at the other men to see if he would have another challenger. The men backed further away from Bolt, looked the other way. No one was ready to take on his fast gun. Not yet anyway.

Bolt walked over to the Mexican who was sprawled on his back next to Batson. Blood spurted from the hole in Chato's chest, formed a red pool beneath him, stained the sawdust crimson. He moaned once. Then his eyes went vacant, stared up at the ceiling without seeing.

The stench of gunsmoke hung in the air.

Two men dead. Needless deaths.

The bartender shuffled back to his station behind the bar. He ordered a young, pimply-faced boy to go for the undertaker.

"When you get back," said Haskins, "bring a bucket of sawdust and a shovel. Get this floor cleaned up."

"You want me to bring the sheriff, too?" asked the gangly boy.

"No need to. It was a fair fight. Chato and Batson drew first. Everyone here saw it." He looked around to see if anyone figured different.

"Drinks on the house, everybody," Lenny announced. "Clem, you and John drag them carcasses outside."

Bolt turned back to the bar, took a sip of his drink. Tom holstered his pistol and joined them. The other men ambled up to the bar to collect their free drinks.

"You've got trouble now," said Lenny as he poured a fresh drink for Bolt and Tom. "Those two ride for the Rocking H. That's Major Horner's outfit."

"Tell Major Horner for us to keep his drunks out of town while we're here," said Bolt.

Out of the corner of his eye, Bolt saw a man leave the bar. He was a short man with slicked-down brown hair, clean shaven. His arms looked too long for his body and he had a slight limp. Wherever he was going, he was in some hurry.

"Likely that'll be done within the hour," said Lenny. "That was the town crier who just left. He runs the supply wagon from Dunfee's General Store out to Horner's ranch."

"He doesn't look like he carries much weight around here."

"Maybe not, but he'll spread the word. They call him the Mouth, but his name's Ferd Moss. Short for Ferdinand."

"Well, I hope the Mouth tells Horner that his boys didn't suffer none. Them was both good clean shots."

CHAPTER TWO

Major Horner stood at the window of his study, gazing out at the vast expanse of his cattle ranch. An unlit cigar dangled from his thick lips. He was a gigantic man with red hair and a bristly red moustache. He was wide shouldered, had thick arms and legs, hands the size of ham hocks.

"Someday, Luke, I'm going to own the biggest cattle empire in the west. It'll stretch from Oklahoma to Texas, to Colorado and Kansas."

"You probably will, the rate you're going." Luke Scarnes was more than Horner's foreman. He was his right hand man, his confidant, his friend. Sometimes Major used him as a sounding board. He was doing that now.

Horner shook his head, strolled back over to his desk, sat down in a padded rocker.

"Right now all I got to worry about is how to get that VeeBee property."

"Them gals don't give up easy." Luke poured a glass of brandy for Major, one for himself.

Scarnes was a hard-jawed man, not as big as Horner, but tall and muscular. A scar creased his

15

eyebrow at a slant, evidence of a pistol whipping he'd gotten several years before. No hair grew on the wide scar, but bushy eyebrows jutted out from either side of it. It made his face look lopsided. Another scar, from the same beating, slashed across his upper lip. He tried to grow a moustache to emulate Horner, but it, too, grew in patches around the scar.

"They can't last much longer."

"Wouldn't think so," said Luke. "We're making it just as rough as we can on them. They'll be happy to sell out before we get through with them."

"I offered them a fair price."

"The problem with them, they don't know they're women. And women aren't supposed to run cattle ranches."

There was a loud knock on the door.

The door burst open before anyone could move to open it.

Moss the Mouth was out of breath.

"Two of your men are dead, Horner," Moss blurted. "I seen 'em killed. At the Pawnee Saloon. Just a few minutes ago. One shot each and they were both dead. Jack Batson and the Mex, Joe Chato."

"Sonofabitch!" Horner got up from his chair, paced across the floor. "Who did it?"

"Strangers in town. A man named Bolt and his partner. Don't know his friend's name. But they were mighty fast on the trigger."

"How'd it happen?" Horner sat on the edge of the wooden desk.

"Batson and Chato were pretty drunk. Swillin' most of the afternoon. I heard 'em talkin' about there being a price on Bolt's head. Next thing I know,

Chato's making rude remarks to this Bolt feller, goading him like. Lenny tried to warn Bolt there'd be trouble if he and his friend stayed, but they wasn't worried. Chato just kept pushin' till the place erupted in gunfire."

"Who drew first?"

"The Mex did. But Batson already had his pistol out of his holster. Had it hidden under the table. Everybody seen it. Bolt and his friend were really fast. If youda blinked your eye, youda missed it."

Anger flared up in Horner, flushed his face as red as his hair. He stood up and fished a five dollar bill out of his pocket, handed it to the babbling man.

"Thanks, Moss. You did right."

Ferd Moss took the bill, stuffed it in his pocket, started to leave. He turned at the doorway.

"Oh, one more thing, Major."

"What's that?"

"Bolt's got a friend in town. A gal who works at the Panhandle Club. Name of Belinda."

Moss walked out of the room, didn't bother to close the door behind him.

"I've heard of Bolt before," said Luke. "He's just a pimp. Owns a couple of whorehouses. One in Abilene, another one in Dodge. He and his partner just got lucky shots, that's all."

Horner went back to his rocking chair, sat down and propped his feet up on the desk. He stroked his moustache, pondered the situation.

"I'm not so sure. Chato and Batson weren't exactly slow. They were two of my best men."

"Yeah, but they couldn't handle their likker. You ____ that."

"Maybe. But Bolt sounds like trouble. I don't like nobody killing my men. Wonder who Bolt knows at the Panhandle. That's where them VeeBee gals work, Belle and Ginny, but I don't know of any Belinda who works there."

"I don't either, and I know 'em all." Luke grinned. "Maybe the Mouth got the name wrong."

"Not Moss. That's one thing about that nosy bastard. When he tells you something, he's got his tally straight."

"Wait a minute. I know who Belinda is. That's Belle. I heard someone at the Panhandle call her that one time."

"Hmmm. I wonder if Belle brought him in to make sure we didn't get her land. Or to give us a hard way to go."

"You want me to send a man in to scout Bolt and his friend out, find out what they want?"

Horner stroked his moustache again, took his feet off the desk.

"No. I want Bolt out of the picture completely."

"You mean . . . ?"

"Yes. He spells trouble. If he's a friend of Belle's, you can bet your sweet ass he's here to help her. I want him to do a disappearing act, you know what I mean?"

"You want to make sure he don't come back."

"You got me. I don't want any of my men involved. Bring somebody else in. Someone nobody knows. Pay him good and make sure he keeps his mouth shut. Don't mention my name. In fact, I don't even want to know who you get. I just want Bolt taken ou Permanently!"

Major looked up as his wife entered the room. "Hello, Elizabeth."

Luke Scarnes gave her a dirty look. He didn't like Major's wife. He thought she was a snoopy bitch who was always sticking her nose in where it didn't belong. Like now. He and Horner were having a private conversation which was none of her business and yet she had just walked right on in without knocking. Of course, the Mouth had left the door open when he left, but that gave her no excuse for barging in like that. If she wanted to see Major, let her do it on her own time.

"Hello, Major," said Elizabeth. "Did I hear you mention a man named Bolt?"

"You know him?" Major's eyebrow shot up.

Elizabeth blushed, the flush rising from her graceful throat, coloring her cheeks. She was a tall, beautiful woman with long blond hair and deep blue eyes. She looked elegant in the long blue gown she wore. A cameo hung from a gold chain around her neck. She always looked elegant, carried herself proudly. Horner saw to that. He spared no expense when it came to buying her clothes and jewelry, trinkets.

"No, it's just an unusual name, that's all."

But Major was suspicious. He had seen her cheeks color. He was even more curious about Bolt than he had been before.

"How come you asked?" said Luke accusingly.

"I just saw Ferd Moss leave and wondered why he was here."

Horner wished he'd been the one to ask her. He knew Luke didn't particularly like Elizabeth. Luke

19

didn't like women, period. But this was Elizabeth's house and she had the right to know what was going on.

"Two of my men were killed," answered Horner. "Moss thought I should know. Bolt was the name of the man who killed them. He's a stranger in town."

"Who was killed?" asked Elizabeth.

"Jack Batson and Joe Chato. Good men. Guess they were likkered up." Major let it go at that.

"I'm sorry, Major. You're busy, I know. I'll see you at supper." She turned and walked out of the room. She climbed the stairs to her bedroom, where she could be alone.

In her room, she sat at her dressing table, in front of the mirror with its ornate sculptured frame, a gift from Major. Idly, she picked up a brush, began preening her long blonde hair.

Yes. She knew Bolt.

But that was before she had married Major.

It seemed like so long ago, but actually it had been less than two years since she'd tangled with Bolt.

She remembered how he used to call her "Betsy," a nickname that wasn't befitting Major Horner's wife. That was when she was the new school marm in Abilene, out on her own for the first time in her life, away from her over-protective father.

She would never forget the day her father came to Abilene. She was a virgin when she met Bolt, but she had fallen hopelessly in love with him and they made love unashamedly out in the woods. He was the most charming man she'd ever known. She could picture him in her mind. His sensuous lips, his blue eyes that stared right at you and said more than he did.

She blushed when she thought about Bolt as her lover. He was far superior to her husband in that department. And, Bolt was her first man. That counted for something.

When she had told her father who she was in love with, her father had exploded with rage, told her she couldn't see him anymore.

That's when she found out who Bolt really was— the owner of a whorehouse and a wanted outlaw. She didn't believe her father until he took her to Bolt's Bawdy House so she could see for herself. She had been so hurt and mad, she really caused a scene that night. Kicking, scratching, cursing. Her father dragged her back home to St. Louis after that. She hadn't seen Bolt since.

That's where she met Major Horner. In St. Louis. She married Horner after a brief courtship. Her father never actually met her husband, but he approved of Major anyway because he was a wealthy man.

She enjoyed her present high station in life as Mrs. Major Horner. It was a respectable position and gave her the security she wanted. Sometimes, she wished Major was more tender in bed, like Bolt had been, but he wasn't and she accepted that fact.

Suddenly, Elizabeth became frightened. Major didn't know about her past and she didn't want him to find out now that she wasn't a virgin when he married her.

She wished Bolt had never come to Black Mesa. She didn't know whether she was afraid because Major might find out or if it was that she was afraid of her own feelings if she happened to see Bolt again. Either

21

way, she wished he would go away.

She had been bitter about Bolt for a long time, still carried a grudge against him, but she didn't want to have him killed.

What was it Major had said when she had entered the study? "I want Bolt taken out—permanently."

She'd have to warn Bolt.

But how? And when?

****

After Bolt and Penrod left the Pawnee Saloon, they registered at the Cimarron Hotel, soaked in a two-bit-a-bath tub. They had supper before they went to the Panhandle Club to look up Belinda Wilkins. It was intermission time when they got there, so Belinda was free.

"Jared, it's so good to see you again!" Belinda threw her arms around Bolt, kissed him on the mouth.

"Nobody's called me that in quite a spell." Bolt grinned at her. "You look even more beautiful than you did before." He stepped back and looked at her. She had slimmed down since he'd last seen her. She looked stunning in her form-fitting green gown. Her spun copper hair was longer now, fell well below her shoulders. Her brown eyes were fawn-like, softer.

"Thanks. So do you. Hi, Tom." She gave Tom a peck on the cheek.

"Tom said you're in trouble, Belinda."

"It's Belle now. Belle Hammond. Hammond's my maiden name. Pretty good stage name, don't you think? I dropped the Wilkins name quick as I could. Yeah, I got big trouble. We stand to lose everything we've got. My partner and me. Come on, let's sit down."

She led them to a table right in front of the stage, waved for a waiter.

"Who's your partner?"

"Ginny. She's a singer here. A dancer, same as me. We put our money together and bought us a small ranch. We're raising cattle, but we're about to lose it all."

"Tom said you were having trouble with cattle rustlers, that you were having a struggle just making ends meet."

"You don't know. It's really been rough. Lucky for me I ran into Tom in Amarillo." She reached over and patted Tom's hand. "I was down there on a cattle buying trip. It was terribly hot that day and I needed something to keep the sun off me. I went into the general store to buy a sun bonnet . . . well, I looked up and there he was. Tom was in the same store. I couldn't believe my eyes. I've been trying to find you ever since you left Abilene, but I lost track of you."

"Fill me in on what's happening now," Bolt said.

"Would you two excuse me?" said Tom. He could see that the conversation was going to drag on. Belinda always was long winded. Besides, he had spotted a glitter gal who interested him. He'd been a long time without a woman.

"Go ahead, Tom. See you later," said Bolt. "Go ahead, Belinda."

"It's a long story. I don't want to talk about it here. I've got one more number to sing. Then we can go

23

someplace and talk."

The band members wandered up on the stage, began tuning up their instruments. Customers shifted in their chairs so they could watch the entertainment. The band struck up a tune. A man dressed in a black suit stepped to the front of the stage.

"And now," said the announcer, "the Panhandle Club presents the fabulous Virginia Darling."

"That's Ginny," Belle whispered. "My partner."

Virginia strolled on stage, smiled down at the men in the audience. She was striking in the long red gown that clung invitingly to her hourglass figure. A slit up the side of the gown showed her long legs off to advantage. Her hair was dark brown. It fell gracefully about her face.

The band played an introduction. She came in on cue, began singing a ballad. Her voice was low and sensuous.

Bolt was stunned by her beauty. Something twisted in his stomach when she smiled. He sat motionless, studying her features as the tempo of the music picked up.

He wasn't the only man in the saloon who was affected by her sensuality. Men leaned forward, goggle-eyed, panting, as she sang the sad love ballad. Every man in that room felt that she was singing just to him. Ginny had that special quality: to make each man feel unique, important. Eye contact, a teasing smile, a wiggle of the hips when she walked slowly around on the stage. These were the things the customers loved about Virginia Darling.

The slit in her long tight skirt was the thing that

drove Bolt crazy. Every time she took a step, she moved her leg in a suggestive circle, exposing her long graceful thigh. He could see right up to her privates when she did it. It was enough to make any man cream his jeans.

The applause was ear-shattering when she finished her song. One more teasing show of her bare leg brought boisterous shouts and whistles from the crowd.

"She's terrific, isn't she?" Belle said.

"She's great," said Bolt.

Belle didn't much like the look in Bolt's eye. She knew what he was thinking.

"Don't worry, Bolt, you couldn't get into Ginny's pants with a full month's pay."

CHAPTER THREE

Belle called Ginny over to their table after she finished her second number.

"Ginny, I'd like to have you meet my friend, Jared Bolt. Bolt, this is Ginny."

"Pleased to meet you, ma'am," said Bolt.

"I've heard a lot about you," said Ginny. She didn't smile. She didn't like to be called "ma'am." It made her sound so old.

"All good, I hope," said Bolt.

Ginny didn't say anything. She also didn't like cocky men. In fact, she didn't like men at all anymore. Not since she had left her husband. He had treated her badly, beating her, making her a slave in her own house. She tolerated men, but she didn't let them get too close to her anymore. Men were all the same anyway. They only wanted one thing from a woman and she wasn't about to give them that satisfaction.

"I've got to dash," said Belle. "I'm on next. You two get acquainted while I do my song. When I'm through we can go someplace where it's a little quieter."

"I enjoyed your singing," Bolt said after Belle was gone. "You were good."

"Thanks," she said.

"How'd you and Belle meet?"

"We met here."

"How long you been in Black Mesa?"

"A year."

It was obvious he wasn't going to be able to engage Ginny in conversation. Now he knew what Belle had meant by her remark about not getting into Ginny's pants. He couldn't even get her to talk to him.

Bolt was relieved when Belle started singing. At least he wouldn't have to have a one-sided conversation.

When Belle finished her song, she grabbed her sweater off a chair and came back to the table.

"You two ready to go?" she asked.

"I'll stay here," said Ginny. "We only have a half an hour before we sing again. You go on. I'm sure you have a lot to talk about. Take your time, Belle. I'll cover for you if you don't get back in time."

"Thanks, Ginny. Come on, Bolt. Let's get out of here."

****

"It's been a nightmare," said Belle. "I'm about to give up. So's Ginny. Only thing is, I don't know where I'd go."

Fully clothed, Bolt stretched out on top of the bed in Belle's room at the Cherokee Hotel.

"I thought you'd be married by now. You were so hell bent on getting married back in Abilene."

"I haven't landed in one spot long enough. Besides, I'm not ready to settle down until I find the right man. You spoiled me, Bolt."

"Did you ever get your uncle's inheritance?"

"Yes, but that's long gone. I tried to find you, but you just disappeared. Judge Wilkins has hounded me until I spent all my inheritance money staying one step ahead of him. I had to become a saloon singer when I got to Black Mesa just to make ends meet."

"I'm sorry it's been so rough. I feel responsible for your troubles. If I hadn't killed your husband, and later his brother, you'd still have your uncle's money. You wouldn't have to work in that saloon."

"Bolt, if you hadn't killed Reed, he'd have killed you. You know that."

"But if I hadn't been with you, there would have been no reason for him to want to kill me."

"No, but I had already left him. He wanted my inheritance in the worst way. He'd have probably killed me to get it if he had to. I couldn't live with him anymore. He was a bad man."

"Judge Wilkins is still after me, too, for killing his sons. I know how you feel. Now, start from the beginning and tell me about the trouble you're having. I'll see if I can help you."

"Ginny and I pooled the little money we had and bought a small ranch. We both want to get out of the dance hall business and live on our ranch all the time. Raise our cattle. We're just working at the saloon until the ranch starts paying for itself. We love the ranch, the work. Or did. The way things are going lately, we're losing money hand over fist."

"How so?"

"We're losing cattle every day. Major Horner's doings, we're sure."

"I've heard the name. Tangled with a couple of his boys this afternoon."

"At the Pawnee?"

"Yair."

"I heard about it. Horner will be out for your hide for that."

"So what's Horner's gripe with you?"

"Horner's got the biggest ranch around. Only problem is, my property cuts right through the middle of his land. When he first bought his property, it was small. He bought out the other ranchers, including the place on the other side of me. Now he wants mine. The Cimarron River makes a bulge at the point where our property joins Horner's. Ginny and I actually control a good part of the river frontage along the extended horseshoe and Horner's got none of it. He has tried to buy our property, but we won't sell to him. It was after that that our cattle started disappearing. We put up barbed wire, but someone cuts it and run Horner's cattle on the VeeBee ranch."

"What's the V B stand for?"

"Virginia and Belle. We've been threatened by Horner's foreman, Luke Scarnes. And his hired men. They've given us a hard time, too."

"Gunnies?"

"Uh huh."

"We'll ride out to your ranch tomorrow, see what we can do to help."

"Oh, it's hopeless." She sat down on the edge of the

bed, looked over at Bolt.

"Nothing's hopeless."

"You always were calm."

"Not always," he grinned.

She looked at his sensuous lips, his clear blue eyes.

"You've always had that same look in your eyes, too," she sighed.

"What look's that?"

"That . . . that hungry look. God, I used to get jealous when you were with another woman. I've grown up a lot."

"Yeah, you were real fiesty."

"I've missed you, Bolt. I've thought a lot about you this last year. Wondered where you were, what you were doing, if you ever married."

"I've been collecting whore houses."

"Bolt, you're crazy. You still do things to me."

"What kind of things?"

"You know." Her voice was husky. She leaned over and kissed him. Passionately. She pressed her body against his, crushed her firm breasts into his chest. She ran her hand inside his shirt, rubbed his bare chest. She brought her hand out, let it glide down to his crotch where she felt the bulge.

"It's still there, Bolt. I want you. Very much."

Bolt felt the warmth of her hand through the cloth of his trousers. His manhood began to stiffen, strain against the material. He responded to her kiss, darted his tongue inside her damp mouth. He grabbed her shoulders, pulled her close.

"You're quite a woman."

She pushed away from him, started unbuttoning his shirt.

30

"You want me, don't you?" she said.

"Yes, I do."

She rose and disrobed, got back in bed, waited for Bolt to undress.

They came together naturally. Bolt rolled over on his side, snuggled close to her soft, yielding body. He found a spongy breast, cupped his hand around it, squeezed it. His kiss was warm and moist on her eager lips. She pushed her tongue deep inside his parted lips. Bolt's tongue flicked in and out, rubbing against hers.

Belle's hand slid down across Bolt's hairy chest, his smooth, firm stomach, down to his crotch. She took his rigid cock in her hand, squeezed it, felt it twitch.

"You're the best. The biggest," she whispered as she nibbled on his ear lobe. Her hot breath and wet tongue lapping at his ear increased the desire that stirred in his loins.

She stroked his bone-hard cock, clasping it firmly in her hand. She moved her hand up and down the length of his erection, sliding the taut skin up over the sensitive mushroom head. She dabbled her finger in the sticky fluid that oozed from the slit eye, smeared it around.

Bolt dipped his head down to her breast, suckled a nipple until it was acorn hard. Her body squirmed against his as she became more aroused. He took the other breast in his hand, held it while he laved the nipple with the tongue. A squeal of delight escaped her lips.

"Yes, I want you," he husked as he moved back up to kiss her inviting lips. He felt a surge of desire as he placed his lips on hers. He closed his eyes, ran his hand down to her bare thighs.

The image in his mind was not of Belinda.

It was of the long provocative legs of Virginia Darling, showing through the slit of her long red gown. Ginny had set his fires to boiling back at the saloon and he couldn't get her out of his mind. Not even when he was so close to Belle.

Belle spread her legs, thrust her hips upward, encouraging his playful touch.

He slid his hand around the smooth bare flesh of her inner thighs. He thought about Ginny.

His hand sought her furry mound, cupped it. He felt the delicate folds of her sex with a searching finger. Her lips were damp and inviting. He spread the lips open, slid his finger along the slippery entrance.

He still thought about Ginny.

His finger slipped inside the warm damp sheath. He pushed in deep. She thrust her pussy up to meet him, stroked his shaft faster.

"I want you inside me. Put it inside," she begged.

Bolt moved over on top of her, his manhood aimed at her sex cleft. She spread her legs wider to accept him. He lowered himself, touched her soft labia with his stiff erection. He slid into her sheath, pushed it in deep until he filled her up. He felt her squirm beneath him.

He penetrated her deeply, felt tight muscles clasp his manhood. He moved in and out of her warm sheath slowly, dipping into her honeypot.

"Bolt, I want to get on top of you. You mind?"

"Be my guest."

Rolling over on his back, he kept his shaft buried

deep inside her. As they tumbled to their new position, Bolt got a whiff of the jasmine toilet water Belle wore. It mingled with the musk of their lovemaking, added to his excitement.

Skewered on his manhood, Belle sat on top of Bolt, began rocking back and forth. She squirmed around until his spear rubbed against her clitoris, massaging it with every stroke. The delicate friction eroded away at her senses until she erupted in orgasm, again and again.

"That feel good?" she said.

"Ummmm."

Bolt lay flat on his back, stimulated by her expert manipulations. He reached up and grabbed a firm breast in his hand. He massaged it, tweaked the nipple to hardness. He felt her muscles tighten around his organ, pull on it as she bobbed up and down. She was like a wild tiger wrestling with its prey.

He felt his juices begin to bubble up, knew he was nearing his own climax. When he could no longer hold back, he rolled her back over so he was on top. He felt her bare thighs against his own, smelled her sweet scent.

He closed his eyes, kissed her passionately.

The image of Ginny flashed through his mind again.

He stroked her deep and quick. It took only a few strokes for him to reach a climax. He hunched forward, held her tight as his sperm spurted through his spear, splattered against the soft lining of her sheath. His mind soared to the pinnacle where he saw everything. Where he saw nothing.

After a moment, he rolled off her, relaxed on the bed while Belle began to dress.

"I'm always just a beat behind you, aren't I, Jared?"

"Huh?"

"Out of step. You move pretty swift."

"I don't understand."

"I mean you were distracted."

"Aw, come on, Belinda. I mean, Belle. You gonna just sneak up on it or go on and open up the door?"

"You'd rather be with Ginny right now, wouldn't you?"

Bolt looked up at Belle, grinned self-consciously. He got up from the bed, stepped into his Levi's.

"Well, now, you put it plain, don't you?"

"You said you wanted it that way. No beating around the bush."

He put his shirt on, buttoned it up, then brushed imaginary lint from it.

"Trouble is, I'm glad to be with you, but I don't deny that Ginny's right prime." He glanced over at Belle to see her reaction.

He felt it coming. He saw her face flush with anger. She set her jaw, bore into him with dark, flashing eyes. She flipped her copper hair defiantly, marched right up to him, put her hands on his shoulders and gave him a healthy shove.

He wasn't expecting it and he toppled backwards, ended up sitting on the edge of the bed.

"You're a no-good, woman-chasing jackass! You're nothing but a conceited, arrogant, egotistical idiot! You think you're God's gift to women! Well, I got news for you. . . ."

"No need to get your dander up," he grinned.

"I'll get my dander up if I damn well please. It's about time someone took you down a notch or two. You expect women to fall all over you, give in to your demands."

"I don't demand nothing."

"No, but you turn on your charm and draw the women to you like flies. You lure them into your trap."

"Can't help it if I'm charming."

"Oh, you . . . you stuck-up jerk! You got calluses on your hand from patting your own back. You can't keep your pecker in your pants."

"Didn't see you complaining a few minutes ago."

"Well, you're . . . you're just no good. You're evil."

He stood up, held her at arm's length as she flailed her arms at him.

"You know, you're pretty when you're mad."

"Don't pretty me, you horny toad."

"My, ain't we in a sod-pawin' mood. You're as tetchy as a teased rattler."

"I've never known anyone like you. You think you can take advantage of women and get away with it."

"Never took advantage of no woman. Thought you said you wasn't jealous no more."

"I'm not," she pouted. "It's just that . . ."

"Come on, now, settle down." He pulled her close to him, patted her on the bottom.

She allowed him to hold her in his arms for a few moments while she calmed herself down. It was true, she knew. Bolt was a charming man. He did attract the pretty women, just by being himself. She thought she'd gotten over her jealousy, but facing it now was something different than just thinking about it. Finally, she pulled herself away from him.

"Well, try for Ginny, if you want," she said sarcastically. "I've watched men break their heads trying to get through that stone wall she puts up. Like I said, you couldn't get into Ginny's pants with a full month's pay."

To Bolt, that was a challenge he couldn't ignore.

Only thing was, he didn't pursue a woman. If it happened, it happened.

Simple as that.

CHAPTER FOUR

Belle was waiting on the porch when Bolt and Tom Penrod arrived at the VeeBee Ranch the next day. She was wearing her work clothes, blue jeans and a blue flannel shirt. She seemed nervous, upset.

"Oh, Bolt. I'm glad you're here. We had a bad time after I went back to the saloon last night. Horner's foreman, Luke Scarnes, was at the saloon with a couple of his hired guns. They heckled Ginny while she was singing, really gave her a bad time. Then when we left the saloon after work to go to our hotel, they were waiting for us. They threatened us. Said we'd better get out of town."

"Horner's trying to scare you off. He's just throwin' dust in the air."

"Well, he's doing a good job of it." She shook her head, wrung her hands. "Do you boys want some coffee?"

"Not now. We'd like to look over the ranch. See what the lay out is."

"Ginny's fixing lunch for us. She'll have it ready when we get back. I'll get my horse and show you around."

They followed her to the stable where she saddled Kelley, her chestnut.

"How big's your spread?" asked Bolt.

"Ginny and I own twelve hundred acres."

"That's a healthy chunk of land," said Tom.

"All prime land, too," said Belle. "We paid fifty cents an acre for it. Bought it from a man named Milt Banks. We didn't find out until after we bought the property why Banks sold out. He was driven off by death threats."

"Horner?"

"Yes. He made it tough for Banks. We thought it was a personal grudge between the two men. But we found out different. Horner wants this land in the worst way."

"Why?" asked Tom.

"Because of the way it's situated. Horner owns a lot more land than we do, but our property cuts his right in half. And the Cimarron River winds around in a horseshoe so that most of it's on our property. I'll show you that later."

"So Banks just gave up," said Bolt. "Why didn't he sell out to Horner?"

"I think Banks sold to us just to spite Horner. To make sure that Horner didn't get this piece of land."

"Don't you and Ginny have any help running the ranch?" asked Tom.

"We've had hired help, but none of the men stay long. Not since one of them was killed in town. We can't prove Horner's men killed him, but we've got our suspicions."

"You got the land for a fair price," said Bolt.

"Ginny and I thought it was a good deal. We want

to quit the saloon business, the song and dance routine, and devote our energies to running a successful cattle ranch. I guess men don't much like the idea of women raising cattle for market, but it's what we want to do. But it's been nothing but trouble. We're about to lose our camisoles.''

She led them through brush, up and over a small hill, to the pasture.

''That's all that's left of our herd.'' She pointed to a group of nine longhorns grazing in the pasture that was enclosed by a fence.

''How many did you have?''

''We'd built the stock up to almost a thousand. But, they've gradually disappeared.''

''Horner throws a mighty big loop, don't he?'' said Tom.

''We don't have enough money to replenish our stock. Come on, I'll show you something else.''

She kicked her horse to action, led them over to a fence line.

''We've spent a small fortune on this Glidden's barbed wire. But every time we check it, we find where it's been cut. We can't afford to keep stringing it, just to have it cut again.''

''Horner?''

''Horner and his men, we're sure. We've seen his cattle on our land. He just cuts the fence and runs his cattle over here, takes some of our cows while he's at it.''

Belle led them up to a butte above the Cimarron River where they could get a good view of the surrounding land.

''See how the Cimarron makes a bulge down there,

kind of an extended horseshoe. It comes way up into our property so that we actually control a good part of the river. The way it winds around, it doesn't touch any part of Horner's land. That's why he wants our property. He tried to talk us into selling to him, made us several offers, but we turned him down. Since then a couple of his men have given us some trouble at the saloon like they did last night. They've heckled us and humiliated us while we're working until we can't stand it any longer. And then threatening us like they did last night. We're ready to quit."

"Never give up," said Bolt. "Sometimes things seem impossible. Like tryin' to scratch your ear with your elbow. But don't worry. We'll figure something out."

When they got back to the ranch, they went inside, smelled the beef cooking.

Ginny greeted them at the door.

"Good morning, Bolt."

"Morning, Ginny. This is my friend, Tom Penrod."

"Hello, Tom. Come on in."

"I heard you sing last night," said Tom. "I enjoyed it."

"Thank you."

Bolt's eyes followed the curves of Ginny's tall body. The Levi's she wore were tight. They clung to her body like a glove, accentuating her long legs and nicely rounded buttocks. Her large breasts strained at the material of her red blouse. Her dark hair was tied back with a ribbon.

"What can we do, Bolt?" asked Belle. "It all seems

so useless."

"What's that?" Her words snapped him out of his trance.

"We've lost most of our cattle. Our money has dwindled away so we don't have enough to replace the cattle. Horner's trying to force us out."

"Horner's rustling your cattle, not because he needs them, but because you do. So, Tom and me and some others we'll hire on, will give a little tit for a little tat."

His eyes bored right through Ginny's bodice when he spoke.

She tanned instantly, then turned bright red under his hot gaze.

"We can't afford a range war," Belle said.

"Well, you got one already. Only thing is, one side is always winning. Let us handle it."

"There's no law in Black Mesa, you know," said Ginny. "Unless it's Horner's law. He carries a lot of weight around here." She turned and walked toward the kitchen.

Bolt sensed Ginny's hostility toward him. She acted as if Bolt was interfering with her life.

"Need some help, Ginny?" Belle called.

"No thanks. It's all ready."

She served a simple, but hearty meal of beef stew and hot biscuits.

"You're a pretty good cook, Ginny," Bolt said when he finished eating. He stared at her with cool, blue eyes.

She glared back at him.

"Yes, I am," she said coldly.

Belle was right about Ginny, Bolt thought. Frosty

as ice toward men. She had a thick wall around her that would be hard to penetrate. Too bad such a lovely creature judged all men by her former husband. Well, let her keep her wall. Bolt had no intention of wasting his time trying to pursue her. He didn't believe in chasing after it.

"Were your cattle branded, Belle?" Bolt asked.

"Most of them were, except for all the calves we had. We never had time to brand them before they were stolen."

"Think the best thing would be for Tom and I to move into the ranch house, if that's all right with you girls. We can work better from here, keep our eyes on things."

"That would be fine, I'm sure," said Ginny sarcastically. "Belle and I generally stay in the Cherokee Hotel on working nights anyway. We ride out in the daytime to do the ranch chores. We're off Sunday and Monday nights and spend those nights out here, but I'm sure we can manage." There was a chill in her voice, a peculiar hostility.

Her tone made Bolt wonder.

****

By the following morning, Bolt and Penrod had signs posted all around the VeeBee Ranch.

NOTICE: ANY COWS ON VEEBEE PROPERTY IS VEEBEE PROPERTY. Signed Jared Bolt, Foreman.

"That oughta let 'em know where we stand," Bolt said as he tacked up the last sign at the far end of the VeeBee Ranch.

"Yair," said Tom. "That should drum up some business."

It wasn't long before the message on the signs was put to a test.

Bolt and Tom were riding back to the ranch house after posting their signs when Bolt spotted the cattle. He and Tom were on a hill, riding close to the fence line. They had just topped a rise when Bolt reined back on his horse, held a hand in the air as a signal for Tom to stop. Tom pulled his horse up alongside Bolt.

"There's our first customers," Bolt said in a low voice.

Slowly, they moved their horses over so their profiles were lost in the shadow of the trees. They watched as one of Horner's men studied the message on the sign Bolt had tacked up, then prodded the cattle on through the broken fence. Three other cowhands surrounded the cattle once they were on VeeBee property and prodded them toward the river.

"Guess the dumb bastard can't read," said Tom.

"That's all right. We just bought ourselves about a hundred healthy cows. Give 'em a chance to get well inside the boundary before we claim what's ours."

Bolt slipped his Winchester out of its sheath, placed it across his lap. He motioned for Tom to do the same.

"You aim to kill 'em?" asked Tom.

"Hell no. I want them alive to carry our message back to Horner."

Horner's men herded the cattle along the path, then vanished from sight into the tree-lined valley below. The sound of hoof beats kept Bolt posted on their location.

"Let's hit it. Now!" Bolt led his horse down the hill, through the brush to the road that Horner's men had used to drive the cattle to water.

They rode along the path, rounded a blind corner. Bolt froze when they came around the bend.

Waiting for them were two of Horner's men, sitting their horses. Bolt almost ran smack dab into them. One of the men was a big, barrel-chested man with a full, dark beard covering his round face. The other one was a kid, no more than eighteen or nineteen years old. The younger man had a rifle leveled at them. Their horses were positioned so they blocked the road.

"You must be the new foreman, Jared Bolt." The voice was deep and husky, threatening. It came from the barrel-chested man, Buster Burlison.

"You called it right," said Bolt.

Tom eased his horse up alongside Bolt, on his right.

"You fellers are stickin' your nose in where it don't belong," said the husky man.

"I reckon you read the sign, unless you're too dumb to read," taunted Bolt.

"See we got us a smart-Alec." Buster's hand hovered above his holster.

Out of the corner of his eye, Bolt saw a third man move in on them. The man stayed off to one side, on Bolt's left. Sunlight bounced off the shotgun he held in his hands.

On the outside, Bolt remained calm and cool. His fingers tightened ever so slightly around the trigger grip of the rifle across his lap. His muscles tensed with an impulse to shoot first and ask questions later. He knew they were in a tight spot. One wrong move and he'd be full of lead. He'd have to play it by ear, push his point as far as he dared.

"You boys is trespassin'," said Bolt calmly. "I think you'd better leave the same way you came."

"Talks tough, don't he," said the thin, slovenly kid.

"Yeah, Sammy. Makes you shake in your boots, don't he?"

The third man, Johnny Von, glared at Bolt with steely eyes, but never said a word.

"You'd better get out of here while the gate's still open," threatened Bolt. "And thanks for returning some of the cattle you rustled."

"Them is Horner's cattle," said Buster. He was becoming angry, agitated, Bolt noticed.

"I doubt that. But, they belong to the VeeBee Ranch now. You saw the sign."

"Like hell they do."

Buster went for his pistol.

Sammy raised his rifle, took aim.

Bolt saw the shotgun jerk slightly as Von started to fire.

Quickly, Bolt leaned to the left in his saddle, brought his right leg up. The rifle resting in his lap tipped at an angle, the barrel pointing toward the ground.

Bolt squeezed the trigger. The bullet went where Bolt wanted it to. It spanged into the ground, kicking up loose dirt a few inches in front of Von's horse. The horse spooked, reared up, his front hooves scratching at empty air.

Von fired just as his horse bucked. The shot cracked the air, was high and wild.

Tom raised his rifle and fired a split second after Bolt did. His bullet whizzed in between Buster and the grimy kid, close enough to startle them.

Sammy brushed at his cheek to make sure the bullet hadn't hit him. By the time he fired, he was too late.

Buster had his pistol almost clear of leather before he decided to use his rifle instead. He lost precious seconds in the switch.

Bolt shot again at the ground, kept Von's horse dancing.

Tom fired twice more, once on either side of the two men who braced them. It was enough to keep them confused.

Bolt leaned forward, threw his head against his horse's neck. He kicked him in the flanks and shot through a narrow space between Buster and the boy. Once through, he reined left and brought his horse to a halt right behind them.

Tom moved quickly, spurring his horse around Buster's right, dropped slightly behind Bolt.

Johnny Von waved the shotgun, trying for a quick shot. But he couldn't get it. His friends, Buster and Sammy, were now in between him and his targets.

Sammy tried to turn his horse around. In the cramped space, he bumped into Buster who was forcing his horse to pivot.

"You dumb ass!" Buster yelled at the kid. "Out of my way!"

Sammy tried to back his horse away from Buster's. It balked, bumped into the other horse again. The horses became agitated with the commotion.

"You fumble fuck!" Buster screamed.

Bolt fired in the air which added to the confusion. Von spurred his horse, rode around his two bumbling companions. He fired at Bolt. Missed because Sammy's horse bumped his.

Sammy was completely bewildered. And scared shitless. He just wanted to get the hell out of there. He spurred his horse in the flanks, took off for the break in the fence. He never looked back. He didn't stop until he was well onto Horner's property.

Bolt shot Von before he could fire again. Blood spurted out of Von's biceps, stained his shirt sleeve. He dropped the shotgun as pain seared his shooting arm. He grabbed his arm with his other hand, tried to force his hand toward his pistol. It was no use. The pain was too great. He looked down, saw the blood ooze through his fingers, trickle down his arm. He realized he had no choice but to get out. He took off, hunching forward in the saddle. He turned his head and yelled at Bolt.

"You fuckin' bastard! I'll kill you for this!"

Bolt whirled around, faced Buster. His rifle was leveled at the heavy man's chest.

"You want to leave on your own, or do you want to go out of here strapped to your horse, toes down?" Bolt said, his blue eyes narrowed.

Buster could face down two men. He'd done it before. But he knew he didn't stand a chance this time.

"We'll be back," Buster threatened as he kicked his horse to a gallop. When he was ten feet away, just before he went around the bend, he swung around in the saddle, fired one more shot. The bullet clunked into a tree behind Bolt.

"Tell Horner we mean business!" Bolt shouted after him.

Bolt's ears buzzed as the air became quiet.

He had almost forgotten about the fourth man who had helped herd the cattle through the broken fence. The one who had driven the cattle on down to the river.

He heard the hoof beats now. Coming up behind him.

CHAPTER FIVE

The man was solid muscle.

J. D. Walters was almost six feet tall; was perfectly coordinated; an expert horseman. His horse was like an extension of his own body. He was dressed in black, from his boots right up to his Stetson.

His rifle was already out of its sheath.

He heard the gunfire from down by the river. Quickly, he rode to the point where he could assess the situation. He was twenty-five feet behind the two VeeBee men who were partially blocking the only path that led out of there. He saw that his own men were gone.

With a slight pressure from J. D.'s knee, the horse knew what was expected of him. In a burst of speed, the horse carried J. D. like a dark streak, straight between Bolt and Penrod.

J. D. cracked off a couple of shots as he approached the two men. He ducked his head as he went between them and then whirled around and shot twice more. The last two bullets were too close for comfort.

Bolt felt the rush of air as one bullet whistled by his cheek. The other one tore a chunk out of Penrod's hat brim, sent the hat spinning in the air.

Bolt and Tom responded by squeezing off quick shots of their own. Tom's bullet was high, over the dark man's head. But Bolt's bullet caught J. D. in the calf of his left leg. It went through the fleshy part, exited the other side, leaving a nice neat hole in the man's leg. Bolt heard the man scream, knew he had hit him.

J. D. paused at the broken fence line just long enough to reach down and snatch the warning sign from the fence post. A few minutes later he caught up with the other three cowhands. They rode somberly back to Horner's ranch house.

****

The men gathered in the kitchen of the Rocking H Ranch. Horner, Scarnes, the four men who had just returned from the VeeBee Ranch. Several of the hired hands followed them into the kitchen to see what had happened.

Horner checked the two men who were wounded, had Elizabeth make temporary bandages from a torn sheet.

"Abe, ride into town and get the doctor. Tell him to come out here," Horner ordered one of the men.

Horner ran a large hand through the thick mass of red hair, shook his head. He looked down at the poster J. D. had given him, then looked around at the four men who sat stiffly in straight chairs.

Three of them stared at the floor, their heads hung. Only Johnny Von looked directly at Horner. They knew they were in for a tongue lashing.

"I don't understand it," Horner boomed. "There's four of you and you couldn't even handle two jaspers between the lot of you. You're supposed to be good. That's why I hired you. Two of you come back here limpin' like wounded pups and the other two of you with your tails tucked between your legs. What's the matter with you? Where are your balls? And, you give away a hundred of our best cattle, to boot!"

"We'll get the cattle back," stammered Buster Burlison, trying to ease the tension.

"You'll do shit!" hollered Horner, his face flushed red with anger. "I don't trust you anymore! It's beyond me how you got yourselves in a mess like that. You dumb assholes are lucky you still got your hides."

"But, after we read that poster, we wanted to make sure the cattle were safe. That's why we sent J. D. on with the herd and the others of us held back to stop that new foreman and his partner," offered Buster. He twisted nervously in his chair.

"Yeah, we had 'em going," grinned Sammy.

"Going, my ass! They saw you coming, you chicken shits."

"I faced 'em alone," bragged J. D. "I had to ride right between the two of 'em and they both had rifles on me. I really outsmarted 'em."

"Then how come you got a hole in your leg if you was so damned smart?"

"Well, I'm still alive."

"Yeah, you got real lucky. When you saw the poster, you should have reported to me. I make the decisions around here. You had no business risking my cattle like that. You should have stayed the hell

51

away from the VeeBee property."

"And have Bolt think we're ascared of him?" Buster pouted.

Horner looked at him with disgust. He strolled across the kitchen, stroked his moustache, walked back. He stared at Johnny Von.

"What about you, Johnny? You're mighty quiet."

"Don't think you'd like what I have to say."

"Let's hear it. Spit it out!" he said impatiently.

"I think you got trouble. More trouble than you bargained for. Those new men over at VeeBee's are tough. And smart. I think they could have wiped out all four of us. Easy. But they didn't. It was like they were playing with us. Cat and mouse. You know."

"What makes you say that?"

"I watched them. Real careful. They had plenty of chances to kill us. They shot high or low. On purpose."

"You think so?"

"Damn right. It was no accident they let us get away. They winged me, but it could have been a gut shot just as easy."

"Don't make sense."

"Why not? They got what they wanted. They kept the cattle. Ran us off. They made their point. Bolt said to tell you they meant business. He also said to thank you for returning some of the cattle you rustled."

"That dirty bastard!" Horner mumbled. He paced back and forth, his face turning bright red. He didn't like what Johnny Von was trying to tell him and he certainly didn't like his men hearing Johnny undermine his position of power like that. He turned to the men who were listening to Horner's reprimand.

"The excitement's over, men. Everybody out. Back to work. I want to talk to these four privately. Luke, you stick around."

Elizabeth stood at the kitchen counter, her back to the men. She took her time folding the sheet that she had torn strips from to make the bandages. She listened closely to the exchange between her husband and Johnny Von. She respected Johnny because he was the only one besides Luke Scarnes who wasn't afraid of her husband. Most of the men were afraid of Major because of his size and his temper.

"I think you're wrong," said Horner after the other men were gone. "Bolt's not bashful about killing a man from what I've seen."

"They're standing their ground," said Johnny. "They're showing you they won't be pushed. It was a smart move on Bolt's part. Not killing us."

"But why wouldn't they kill you if they had the chance?"

"Maybe they just didn't want to kindle your wrath." Von brought his hand up and rubbed his nose. It covered the smile on his lips. It gave him a sense of satisfaction to see the big man squirm.

"Didn't seem to bother him none when he killed Batson and Chato."

"That was a different story, and you know it. Batson and the Mex were troublemakers. Drunk, too. They got what they deserved."

That stung. Anger flushed Horner's cheeks again. He didn't like anyone putting down his men, even if it was one of his own men.

"I'd like to take care of Bolt personally," said Von,

pushing a point. "To settle a score."

"No!" boomed Horner. "I'll handle it myself." He turned away from Von. "You boys can wait here until the doctor comes. Come on, Luke." He jammed his hands in his pocket and stalked out of the room.

Elizabeth waited a few minutes and then tiptoed down the hall, stopping outside Major's study.

She could just barely make out the conversation behind the closed door.

****

"Well, we won round one," said Tom, recovering his hat from the ground. He spun the hat in his hands. "And old John B's worth more with a hole in the brim."

"Keep that up, you're gonna have to get yourself some bonnet strings," Bolt laughed. "Yeah, what a bunch of clumsy oafs."

"Wonder how Horner's taking it."

"I'll bet he's horning the brush by now. Come on, let's get those cattle, move them up to the pasture."

The cattle were scattered. Some were drinking at the river, others wandering aimlessly, grazing.

Bolt slid down off his horse, examined the cattle.

"He's been burning rawhide," Bolt said. "These cows are carrying Horner's brand, the Rocking H. But look at this . . ."

Tom swung himself down, joined Bolt.

"He's a brand blotcher, Tom. See here." He pointed to the hide of one of the cows.

"Yep, he's been working the brands, all right."

"He's not even trying to change the brand or

disguise it. He's just blotting out one brand by burning the hide in a block, then applying his own brand next to it."

"Guess he couldn't figure out how to change VB to a Rocking H."

"That's all right. We know who they belong to."

"Look, these calves over here don't have a brand."

"Well, Belle said she hadn't branded her calves yet. Guess Horner didn't get around to it either. We're going to keep the irons hot. Two can play at this game. Come on, let's get these cattle up to the pasture near the house where we can keep a close eye on them. We're going to need some help so we can keep a twenty-four hour watch on them. I wouldn't put it past Horner to make a midnight raid."

They herded the cattle together, headed them toward the pasture, a small grass and brush covered patch of land within the larger grazing area. Located behind the house, opposite the bunkhouse, this fenced land was designed as a holding area for newly acquired cattle. A place to keep the cows until they could be checked and branded before they were let out to the expansive grazing fields.

Bolt rode around the fence line of the twenty-acre pasture to check for breaks. The fence was in good repair, the gate sturdy. The grazing area wasn't enough for that many cows, but it would have to do until they could enlarge the area, extend the fence line.

****

"What was all the shooting about?" Belle asked

when Bolt and Tom walked up to the house.

"Just a little target practice," said Bolt.

"Oh?"

"Yeah. You and Ginny are richer by a hundred head."

"You joshing me?"

"Go look for yourself."

She threw her arms around Bolt's neck.

"Oh, Bolt, that's great!" She stepped back, anxious to hear the details. "How'd you manage that?"

"Easy," grinned Bolt. "Horner's men just brought them over and dumped them in our laps."

"Be serious," she said. "What happened?"

"I just told you."

"It's true," said Tom. "We just tacked up a few posters asking people to bring us their cattle and darned if Horner didn't oblige."

"Stop it. Both of you," laughed Belle. "Ginny and I saw the posters when we got here this morning. Come on in and have a cup of coffee."

Ginny poured the steaming coffee, then sat at the kitchen table with the others.

"We're going to need your branding iron," said Bolt. "Where is it?"

"It's in the shed by the bunkhouse. I'll dig it out for you," said Belle.

"Do you have any more barbed wire? We're going to enlarge the small fenced pasture."

"I think there's a roll of it out in the shed. I'll check it."

"Won't be enough," said Tom. "We'll get some more."

"Another thing," said Bolt. "Tom and I decided

we're going to hire a couple of hands to help us. Got any suggestions?''

Belle thought a minute.

"Can't Ginny and I help you?" she asked.

"No. We're going to put a twenty-four hour watch on those cattle. We'll need to put in some long nights."

"I don't know of anyone off hand," said Belle. "Horner controls most of the men in town. The others are afraid to come to work for us. We know. We've tried."

"How about the Gallihans?" said Ginny. "They offered to help us."

"That's right," said Belle. "I didn't think of them."

"Where do I find them?" said Bolt.

"Patrick Gallihan lives up on the hill behind us. He has a son who is about twenty or so. Nice people. I'm sure they'd help us."

"I'll pay them a visit," said Bolt.

"It's kind of tricky getting to their place," said Belle. "You have to cross the river just at the right spot. Otherwise the river runs too deep." She went on to explain where he would have to cross the river, what path he should take once he'd crossed.

"I can find it," he said.

"Sounds like you've got everything under control," Belle said.

"Before we get through, you're going to have three or four thousand cattle. For a start. Shouldn't take us more than a few days."

"You work fast," said Ginny coldly.

Bolt knew she was putting him down for boasting.

Only he wasn't boasting.

"Pretty fast," he said. "That's so we can get back to enjoying life's little pleasures." His eyes bored into Ginny's.

She flushed, hated him for his arrogance.

"You should try it sometime, Ginny. Experiencing the good things in life. You might enjoy it."

CHAPTER SIX

Bolt kept his horse, Nick, on the game trail that dropped down to the Cimarron. The river ran full this time of year. Rocks beneath the rushing water were covered with a green slime.

He paused at riveredge, looking for the shallow crossing Belle had told him about. Up ahead, he saw where the river narrowed, hoped it was the right place. Otherwise he'd have to cross the river twice, as she said, because of the horseshoe the river formed.

Nick stepped gingerly into the fast-flowing river. He picked his way across the slippery rocks, cold water cascading around his legs and chest. Bolt slipped his boots out of the stirrups, brought his feet up high to keep them dry.

Shortly after he crossed the river, Bolt knew he'd taken the right path. He could see the Gallihan ranch perched high atop a hill. The house was nestled among the tall trees that surrounded it.

The horse followed the dirt road that wound around the hill on a gradual slope. Nick slowed down near the top as the road got steeper.

Bolt was almost at the crest of the hill when he

heard the hoof beats. He looked up just in time to see the rear end of a horse disappear around a bend in the road ahead of him.

A black horse. Moving too fast for him to get a glimpse of the rider. It surprised him. He wondered why he hadn't seen it before. He had checked his back trail often, as he always did, and he had kept a keen eye on the road ahead of him as well. The horse had been just a flash of black legs and tail.

He kicked Nick in the flanks, spurring him to a faster pace. It was no use. The horse threw his head in the air, strained to pick up more speed, but the grade was too steep to go much faster.

Bolt wondered where the black horse had come from. Obviously, it hadn't been on the same road Bolt was on. Moving that fast, the other horse would have passed Bolt along the way.

And, who was the rider? One of the Gallihans? One of Horner's men? Maybe there hadn't been a rider at all.

There was no trace of the black horse as Bolt went around the bend in the road. Instead, the Gallihan house loomed up two hundred feet ahead of him.

"Hello the house," Bolt called out when he was thirty yards away.

Patrick Gallihan stepped out on the porch, a Winchester rifle tucked in the crook of his arm. He was a short, rotund man with neatly trimmed sandy hair, green eyes. He held a hand up to shade his eyes from the sun.

"Friend or foe?" He raised the rifle slightly, aimed it in Bolt's direction.

"Friend, Mr. Gallihan. I'm a new neighbor," Bolt

said, moving his horse closer to the porch. "I'm a friend of Belle Hammond of the VeeBee Ranch."

"Come on up, cowboy."

Bolt rode to the hitchrail in front of the porch where he dismounted and looped the reins over the rail.

"The name's Bolt," he said, extending his hand.

"Patrick Gallihan." He lowered the rifle.

"I've been a friend of Belle's for a long time. I'm taking over as foreman of the VeeBee for a spell."

"Come in, come in."

Bolt followed the Irishman inside. Gallihan leaned his rifle in a corner, motioned for Bolt to sit down.

"Caroline, we got company," Patrick called.

Caroline came into the room, wiping her hands on her apron. She was slightly taller than her husband, slimmer, with a nicely rounded figure. She looked much younger than Patrick. Only the way she wore her bright red hair tied back in a bun gave her a look of maturity.

"Caroline, this is Bolt, the new foreman at VeeBee's."

"Pleased to meet you," she said as she curtsied. Her green eyes twinkled as she spoke. Bolt liked her smile. It was genuine, disarming.

"Same here."

"Would you like some coffee?" Caroline asked. "Or brandy?"

"Coffee would be fine."

"Mighty nice of you to call on us," said Patrick when his wife left the room. "We don't get much company up here."

"This ain't exactly a social call, Mr. Gallihan."

"Just call me Paddy, me boy."

"Paddy. The VeeBee Ranch is in trouble. Most of Belle's cattle are gone. Rustled by Horner and his bunch at the Rocking H. They've been giving her trouble at her work, too. She said you might be willing to help us out for a while. For pay, of course."

"I've heard about her troubles. Been going on a good long time. Even before she moved in. Milt Banks was a good neighbor until Horner ran him off. I guess we been blessed with the luck of the Irish. Horner don't bother us. The way we're situated up here makes it mighty inconvenient for him to make us trouble. I wish there was some way Horner could be stopped, but I don't see how. Some say he's the law around these parts."

"He ain't the kingfish he thinks he is. We can stop him, but we'll need some back-up help."

"We'd be obliged to assist you if we can. What do you aim to do?"

"Let me worry about that. Belle says you got a son. We need both of you to help guard the cattle for a few days. Or nights. Can do?"

"Sure. Mike and I'll help. My nephew too. Dennis. He's my brother's boy. Came to live with us a while back. Same age as Mike. Both twenty-two."

"Here's your coffee." The voice was soft, velvet.

Bolt looked up, startled.

"Thanks, honey." Gallihan turned to Bolt. "This is my daughter, Kathleen. Kathleen, meet our new neighbor, Bolt."

"Pleased to meet you," she said politely.

Bolt didn't mean to stare, but he couldn't take his

eyes off the girl. The resemblance to her mother was haunting. They looked enough alike to be identical twins. Only the way Kathleen's red hair fell softly to her shoulders gave her a more youthful look.

As Bolt watched her, he noticed that her green eyes didn't have the same sparkle that her mother's did. And she didn't smile. In fact she seemed cold, almost rude. Perhaps she was just shy. She avoided eye contact with Bolt as she set the tray down on the low table in front of the couch.

Paddy felt the tension in the room.

"Yes siree sir," he said awkwardly. "Horner should mind his own business."

Bolt didn't answer.

Kathleen flushed under Bolt's gaze. She quickly poured the coffee and fled the room.

"That girl is me pride and joy," beamed Paddy when she was gone. "Purty, ain't she?"

"Yes, sir."

"I didn't know she was home yet. She spends most of her time out there riding that goldanged horse of hers. Well, now, where were we?"

"Our cattle count is low right now, but if you and your boys can help us stand guard, we'll be able to keep Horner from rustling any more."

"Wonder why he's never bothered our cattle."

Bolt blew on the steaming coffee before he took a sip.

"Horner don't want Belle's cows. He wants her land. He needs her land. Or the water on it."

"I suppose you're right." Paddy scratched his head, trying to absorb the premise.

"Are the boys around?" Bolt asked.

"Yep. They're out back, doing the chores. When you're through with your coffee, I'll take you out there and introduce you."

Bolt set his empty coffee cup on the table a few minutes later and followed the short Irishman to the corral where Mike and Dennis were watering the horses. There were six horses in the pen, Bolt noticed.

One of them was a big black. It was slick with sweat.

"Your daughter's horse? The black one?"

"Yep. What makes you ask?"

"Just curious."

"Mike. Dennis. This here's Bolt. He's the new foreman over to VeeBee."

Mike wiped his hand across his Levi's before he offered it in a handshake. He stood a couple of inches shorter than Bolt, but taller than his father. A shock of sandy-colored hair fell across his eyes.

Dennis stood a few feet away, his legs spread, hands on hips. He was tall and muscular, with light brown hair and deep blue eyes.

"Bolt's come to ask our assistance and I told him you'd both help out. Horner and his bunch are at it again, giving the VeeBee women a hard way to go. Same's he did to Milt Banks a few months back. Bolt here thinks he can straighten Horner out."

"He needs some straightening," said Dennis. "That dirty bastard."

Bolt was surprised at the young man's outburst. He saw Dennis' cheeks flush with anger, his jaw stiffen.

"You know Horner?"

Dennis looked down, stabbed at the ground with

the toe of his boot.

"Not really. Just by sight and reputation."

"We'll give you a hand," said Mike. "What do you want us to do?"

"Just do some cattle watching for a couple of nights. See that Horner and his men don't get sticky fingers again."

"Sounds simple enough," said Mike.

"Simple enough. Can you men come over after supper tonight? We'll take shifts watching for Horner's men. You can sleep in the bunkhouse when you're not on watch."

"We'll be there," said Dennis.

Bolt turned to Paddy.

"You stay here with your women tonight, Paddy. You can come over in the morning when the boys return."

"That's fair enough," said Paddy, relieved that he wouldn't have to stand a night watch.

****

The emaciated bartender cringed when he saw Bolt stroll through the batwing doors. He lowered his head as Bolt made his way to the bar.

"Beer," Bolt said simply.

As Lenny Haskins poured the beer into a smudgy glass, he thought about the two men Bolt had killed there. He hoped there wouldn't be any more trouble at the Pawnee. He started to say something to Bolt, but thought better of it.

Bolt plunked down two bits, picked up the beer that Lenny shoved at him. He leaned forward, rested his arms on the bar and studied the other customers. He figured he might need to hire more men than just the Gallihans if his plan worked.

It was early afternoon. The crowd was still orderly. If things went as normal, the place would be buzzing with loud drunks and troublemakers in another few hours.

"There's a gentleman wants to buy you a drink." Lenny's gravelly voice broke in on Bolt's thoughts.

"Who?"

Lenny nodded to a table in the corner of the room. "Major Horner," said Lenny.

Bolt glanced over at the table. He would have recognized the big man from Belle's description if Lenny hadn't named him. Horner sat in the chair, a giant hulk of a man. His red hair was properly slicked back. He toyed with an unlit cigar.

Bolt slid off his stool, sauntered over to Horner's table. He carried his beer with him.

Horner looked up when Bolt approached. He made a sweeping gesture with his large arm, motioning for Bolt to sit down.

"I'm Major Horner. Won't you join me for a drink?"

The chair screeched against the wooden floor as Bolt pulled it out, sat down facing the big man. Bolt's face was a mask, hiding the contempt he felt for the power-hungry man.

"I've got my own." Bolt set his glass of beer on the table in front of him.

Horner stuck his hand in the air, waved a pudgy finger to get the bartender's attention.

"I'll buy you another."

Horner ordered another beer for Bolt, a brandy for himself. Lenny shuffled back to the table, a gaudily painted tray advertising Zang's Beer balanced on one hand. The beer sloshed over when he set it down. He wiped it up with a grimy towel. After Horner paid for the drinks, Lenny glared at the two men before ambling back to the bar. It was his way of warning them that he didn't want any more fights or killings at the Pawnee.

"I'm not going to mince words with you, Bolt. I've got a proposition I think you'll be interested in."

Bolt took a sip of beer, peered over the top of the glass, his cold blue eyes boring into Horner. He watched the red-haired man nervously spin the cigar like a pencil in fingers that were every bit as long and thick as the cigar. Horner cleared his throat, then spoke again.

"I know of your reputation. You're fast and you're accurate. I'd like you to come work for me. Top pay."

"I ain't a gun, Mr. Horner. And I don't hire out my reputation."

"Not quite true. You've hired on as a gunnie for the VeeBee Ranch. That I know to be a fact. I'm prepared to offer you more money than they're paying you. I'll double it."

"You don't hear too good. I'll say it again. My gun ain't for hire." Bolt pushed his chair back, started to get up.

"Wait a minute, Bolt. I'll give you a thousand dollars just to leave town and go back to wherever you came from."

"Nope. I kinda like it around here."

Horner's face flushed with anger. He was used to

getting his own way, paying the price when he had to. He stuck the unlit cigar in his pocket, stroked his thick moustache.

"You killed two of my men. I don't like it."

"You should tell your men not to drink in town if they can't handle it."

"And you stole some cattle from me. Rustling is a hanging offense."

"Well, we got plenty of rope. You keep your rustlers off VeeBee land or there's liable to be a lot of cottonwood blossoms along the Cimarron."

Bolt got up and walked toward the batwing doors. He had made his point. There was nothing more to say. Horner stood up and followed Bolt. He was infuriated that the cocky youth hadn't accepted his offer. His patience was wearing thin. He wanted Bolt out of the picture. Now.

Bolt stepped out in the bright daylight, Horner on his heels. He stopped dead in his tracks when he saw the beautiful blonde woman standing on the board-walk in front of him.

He recognized her immediately. Betsy Kendrick. An old friend from Abilene. More than a nodding acquaintance, even though he had only known her briefly. He had thought about her, wondered what had happened to her after her father came to Abilene and whisked her away from the bawdy life. Away from him. She had turned out to be a fiesty one when she found out that he owned a whorehouse and that he was wanted by the law.

She looked elegant now. Evidently she had done well for herself. She was looking right at him. Surely she must recognize him. He stepped forward, was about to say something to her when Horner spoke.

"Elizabeth. What are you doing here?"

"I came in to town to do some shopping, Major. I saw Luke here and your horse, so I thought I'd wait for you, tell you I wouldn't be home for awhile. Anything you need?"

What the hell was going on? Bolt wondered. Could she be Horner's wife? The fancy clothes she wore. The air of wealth about her. The jewels. She couldn't afford those things on a teacher's salary.

The look in her eyes told Bolt not to let on he knew her.

"No, Elizabeth," said Horner. "I'd like to stay and shop with you but I have a lot to do back at the ranch. I'll walk to the market with you and pick up some cigars before I go."

He took a couple of steps closer to his foreman who had been waiting for him. "I'll be right back, Luke."

In that brief moment, Elizabeth walked past Bolt. Close enough to whisper something to him.

"Meet me at the Cherokee Hotel. Half an hour." She walked right on by him toward the store, Horner catching up to her.

Bolt wasn't sure he wanted to meet Betsy at the Cherokee. It could be a set up. After all, Betsy had been furious with him the last time they were together. They hadn't parted on exactly friendly terms. And now, if she was tied in with Horner, possibly his wife . . . well, it might prove interesting.

He made up his mind to meet Betsy.

His curiosity had to be satisfied.

CHAPTER SEVEN

Bolt strode into the Cherokee Hotel, glanced around the lobby. Nobody paid any attention to him. He walked to some empty chairs in a far corner, sat down facing the door. He had been to the Cherokee before.

Two elderly gentlemen sat on a worn sofa. They wore clean but wrinkled clothes. The one who chewed tobacco was missing a front tooth. He spat the brown juice through the gap in his teeth, hitting the brass spittoon on the floor beside him. He had perfected the gesture, very seldom missed the target.

Three other men who stayed at the hotel sat across from them in tattered overstuffed chairs. The old timers talked about the way things used to be before Grant became President. It was a way to pass the idle time. It was a habit with them. They gathered in the lobby almost every afternoon, passing the hours until time for supper.

There were other people in the lobby. Two women sat on straight chairs by a window, resting feet that were sore from shopping. A nicely dressed couple sat with a piece of luggage between them, waiting for the stage. A stranger stood at the desk asking the clerk about a room.

This was where Belle and Ginny had rooms for those nights when they worked at the Panhandle Club until the wee early hours of the morning. On those nights, they came to their rooms, slept late in the morning before going out to the ranch to do the chores. Usually they returned to the hotel about dusk, in time to dress for another night of singing and dancing. It was only on their nights off, Sunday and Monday, that they slept at their ranch. They would be at the ranch now.

Bolt watched the people in the lobby and hoped he'd never get so old that the only thing he looked forward to was sitting in a broken down hotel lobby, talking about the past.

He thought about Betsy and the coincidence of bumping into her again after all these months. From the exchange he had seen between Horner and Betsy, it was obvious that she was Horner's wife.

She was more refined than she had been when he had known her, more elegant. Money would do that to a woman. He just couldn't understand how a girl who was so naïve could get involved with a man like Horner, who was an aggressive, power-hungry thief. Perhaps it was because of her naïveté. Or maybe her father pushed her into a marriage to a man with wealth and power.

He remembered how her father had destroyed his relationship with Betsy by telling his daughter that she was being courted by an outlaw who owned his own whorehouse. Well, both counts were true—to a point. He was a wanted man. Wanted for killing

71

Belle's husband. That was in self-defense. Wanted for taking money that was rightfully his from a bank in Fort Scott.

And he did own his own whorehouse. Two of them. But not for the reasons people thought. Not to have a string of girls at his disposal. In fact, he made a point of never sleeping with the glitter gals. Not the ones who worked for him. Not with the girls who worked for others.

When Elizabeth Horner, nee Kendrick, entered the hotel lobby, the elderly gentlemen turned to stare. A smile crossed Bolt's face. He knew what the old timers were thinking.

Bolt stood up until he caught Betsy's attention. She spotted him, walked in his direction.

Bolt searched her face for some clue to her mood. Finally, she smiled.

"Have a seat." He gestured to the empty chair that faced him.

"Thanks. It's good to see you again." She sat down on the edge of her chair, leaned forward. There was an air of anticipation to her posture.

"How've you been?" Bolt didn't know what else to say. His curiosity was piqued, but he didn't want to pry.

"Fine. But I've got to talk to you."

"Talk away."

She turned her head and looked at the other people in the lobby.

"Not here. Can we go someplace where we can be alone?"

"Sure. I'll take a room here."

Her eyebrows shot up in question marks.

"Well, you want to talk or not?"

"Yes. Of course."

She sat up tall in her chair, nervously brushing a wisp of long blonde hair back away from her face as Bolt walked to the desk. She felt awkward about Bolt getting a hotel room for them even though she needed desperately to talk to him, to say things she couldn't risk anyone hearing.

A strange feeling began to gnaw at the pit of her stomach. The palms of her hands turned clammy. She brought a hand up to her throat, felt the flush that crept up her body. She had experienced that same butterflies-in-the-stomach feeling before. When she had been with Bolt in Abilene. When she was still a virgin.

A few minutes later, she saw Bolt motion to her from the clerk's desk. Why couldn't he have come back to get her instead of waving his fingers in the air? She stood up quickly and marched toward Bolt. She kept her eyes straight ahead, not daring to look at the others in the lobby. She wondered if anyone had recognized her. Not likely, since she didn't know any of those she saw. She felt like a thief, a sneak. Like a kept woman.

She lowered her head when she got to the desk. She followed Bolt to the room, walking a few steps behind him, as if to give the appearance that they weren't together.

Bolt laughed after he closed the door behind them.

"What's the matter? Never been alone in a hotel room with a man before?"

"Not really. Only that once with you."

She wished she hadn't said it, the minute it was out

of her mouth. She had intended not to refer to their brief romantic interlude, but it just popped out.

"It wasn't so bad, was it?" he grinned.

"Bolt, I'm a married woman now."

"Horner?" His face turned serious.

"Yes. That's what I want to talk to you about." She sat down on a straight chair. "Your life is in danger. My . . . my husband wants you out of the way. He's arranged to have a man brought in from another town to kill you."

"Why is he so interested in me?"

"I guess he thinks you're a threat to him getting the land he wants."

"Land that belongs to someone else."

"All he wants is to buy the land legally from the owners of the VeeBee Ranch."

"It ain't for sale. I told your husband that."

"Why don't you just go away, Bolt? It would be so much easier."

"Who's the man he's bringing in to face me?"

"I don't know. I overheard Major talking to his foreman, Luke Scarnes. Major told Luke he wanted an outsider brought in so Major couldn't be tied in with your death. Major doesn't even know who the man is. Luke is making the arrangements. You've got to get out of town."

"Luke the one with the scarred face?"

"Yes."

Bolt walked across the room, sat on the edge of the bed.

"Why are you telling me all this, Betsy?"

"I just don't want to see you killed. I was mad at you for what you did to me, but I wanted to warn you to be careful. Please get out of town. You don't have much time."

"How much time?"

"I don't know. A day, a few days. Luke told Major that the man was a professional killer, but he didn't say where the man was coming from."

"How'd you get tied up with Horner?"

"I met him back in St. Louis at a dinner party."

"Did your father approve of *him?*" It was meant to be sarcastic.

"Actually, Father never met Major because Father was out of town when we had our short courtship. But Father approved of our marriage. He knew of Major's reputation and he figured Major had enough money to provide for me. Not that I care about the money."

"You wear it well, Betsy."

"No one ever called me that except you."

There was that fluttery feeling in her stomach again. A twinge in her loins. Something in the way Bolt said her name turned her legs to jelly. The way he looked at her with those pale blue eyes. His sensual lips when he smiled. She had no business feeling like she did, she knew, but Bolt had that affect on her. Her uncomfortable feeling told her it was time to go. She stood up, took a couple of steps toward the bed, extended her hand.

"I have to get back home now. Please leave town right away."

Bolt stood up, took her hand.

"Thanks for the warning, Betsy, but I won't leave. Not until I've done what I came to do."

"Please, Bolt, please go away. I don't want you

killed. I couldn't live with myself if my husband was responsible for your death." She was on the edge of hysteria. Tears welled up in her eyes, spilled over.

"Don't worry about me," he said softly. He put his hands on her shoulders, drew her close to him. He felt the warmth of her body press against his. His manhood began to harden in its cloth prison. His loins ached for her warm flesh.

She stayed in his embrace for a long moment, struggling with her emotions. It felt good and natural to be in Bolt's arms, but she was afraid to let her guard down. Finally, she lifted her head from his shoulder. She stared into his pale blue eyes.

"Oh, Bolt. I loved you so much."

"I know."

"I wish . . . I wish things could have been different. I've thought about you so much and wish we could have been together forever."

"I'm not the type to settle down, Betsy."

"I suppose not." She hugged him tight, pressed her body into his again. She wanted to stay with him for a long time.

Impulsively, she kissed him on the lips. It was a passionate kiss, full of desire. She wriggled her thighs against Bolt until she felt the bulge of his crotch.

"Bolt, I want you. I didn't think I would, but I do." Her voice was a velvet husk.

"Come here, Betsy."

He took her hand, led her to the bed. Slowly, he unbuttoned the front of her ruffled blue blouse. He slipped the long sleeves down over her pale arms, let the blouse fall to the floor. He removed the lacey camisole she wore under the blouse, exposing her large, creamy white breasts. He cupped one of them in his hand, leaned over, kissed the nipple. He did the same to her other breast. Her passion rose to a peak as her nipples became hard kernels in his mouth.

Bolt stepped back and unbuckled his gunbelt, hung it on the iron bedpost. He flung the bedcovers back. As he started unbuttoning his shirt, Betsy followed his lead, removed the rest of her clothing. She sat on the edge of the bed, then moved over in the middle, sprawling on the clean sheets like an alluring siren. Her blue eyes beckoned.

When Bolt stepped out of his shorts, she saw that he was ready for her. His swollen member jutted upward, the tight skin glistening in the afternoon light. He rolled onto the bed next to her. Excitement flooded through their bodies at the delicate moment when their bare flesh touched.

Bolt kissed her soft lips, parting them with his tongue. She responded with a passion to match his. Her tongue slithered across his as she pressed her smooth body against him. Her breasts crushed against his chest. Her hot thighs rubbed against his as she draped a leg over his legs. She was like a kitten, starved for love and affection.

"You do things to me, Bolt," she panted. "Good things. You make me tingle all over."

"I hope so."

She reached down and took his spear in her hand, folded her fingers around it. She moved her hand up and down its length, felt it pulse under her caress.

Bolt was surprised by her boldness. She was more mature now than she had been that first time he had made love to her. She was more aware of her own sexuality. More sure of it.

Bolt kissed her again, explored her body with his hand. He ran his hand over her firm, nicely rounded breasts, down across her flat tummy, to her smooth inner thighs. She jerked when his fingers touched her furry mound. Her gasp broke the stillness in the room.

"Did I hurt you?"

"Oh, no. It feels so good when you touch me there." Her words encouraged him to massage the swollen lips of her sex. He ran a searching finger across the outside of her slit, felt the dampness of her passion.

"Ummmmm, that's good," she moaned. She thrust her loins upward, increased her stroking of his stiff cock.

Without any warning, Betsy whirled her body around, lowered her head to his crotch. As she squeezed the stem of his erection, she placed her lips on the very tip of the mushroom head. The hard shaft jerked with a quick spasm. Her tongue laved at the lemony honey that leaked from the tiny slit. She pursed her lips to an O, let them glide down over the bulbous head.

Bolt thrust his crotch upward, exulting in her oral manipulations. He felt her warm mouth envelop his sensitive spearhead, felt the warm moisture around it. Her head bobbed up and down as she suckled it like a newborn calf.

Betsy sensed that Bolt was on the thin edge of passion. She knew that if she didn't slow down, it would be too late. She paused before she drew her mouth up the length of his shaft and expelled the organ. She rolled over on her back, spreading her legs in invitation.

"Put it in me now," she begged. "Please."

He positioned himself above her, aimed his rigid shaft and dipped down to touch her pussy. His spear parted her lips, slipped smoothly inside. She gasped as he plunged into her. She shook beneath him as orgasm overtook her.

He pumped into her tight sheath, ramming deep. He knew he was too close to his own ejaculation to last much longer. Her muscles gripped him, sucked him in deeper. He felt his seed begin to bubble up. He stroked her faster, deeper.

And then it was all over. He exploded in the mindless state of convulsive orgasm. He held her tight until all of his milky seed had oozed into her waiting sheath. Finally, when he was limp, he rolled off her.

"Thank you, Betsy. You're a good woman."

"You don't know how good you are, Bolt. I wish . . . I wish . . ."

"I know."

She fought back the tears that were threatening to form.

"I've got to get going," she said. "I've been here too long as it is. Bolt, would you stay here for a little while, let me leave alone? It wouldn't do to have anyone see us leaving the hotel together."

"No problem."

She dressed quickly, grabbed her purse and went to the door.

"Be careful," she said and then she was gone. She

kept her head lowered as she walked through the lobby, out the door. She walked to her horse which was hitched to the rail in front of the bank, two buildings down from the hotel.

Across the street from the hotel, in front of Dunfee's General Store, a short man with slick brown hair leaned against a broom. His beetle eyes were trained on the hotel entrance. He watched Elizabeth Horner step outside from the Cherokee Hotel lobby.

An hour before he had seen her go in the hotel alone.

He didn't know who she had been with, but he didn't figure she'd spent all that time sitting in the lobby.

Moss the Mouth couldn't wait to spread the news.

This juicy bit of gossip was too good to keep to himself. It was downright scandalous that Major Horner's wife was having an affair.

CHAPTER EIGHT

Supper was ready when Bolt returned from town. He still couldn't understand how a sweet, naïve girl like Betsy Kendrick could have married such a ruthless man as Horner. But, as Bolt's father used to preach: "God works in mysterious ways."

Bolt had eaten a light lunch in town, so he was pleased with the spread the girls served.

Shortly after they washed the supper dishes, Belle and Ginny rode in to town to dress for their night's work at the Panhandle Club. They wouldn't come back out to the ranch until late the following morning, after they got a few hours sleep at their hotel rooms.

The Gallihan boys were prompt.

Bolt and Tom Penrod were out at the corral checking the cattle when Mike and his cousin, Dennis, rode up. The evening sky was beginning to pale and a chill set in with the coming darkness.

"Glad you're here," greeted Bolt.

"Gonna be a chilly one," said Mike.

"Yep. Just about time to get a fire started. I got the wood stacked, ready to go. There's plenty of logs cut to keep the fire going all night."

"Good," said Dennis, rubbing his hands together.

"I don't expect any trouble tonight. I doubt that Horner's men will try anything so soon, but I want to be prepared. Just in case."

"I wish Horner would show up himself," said Dennis. "I'd like to nail him to a tree and pump him so full of lead that the weight would tear him apart."

There it was again. Dennis' hostility toward a man he barely knew.

Bolt wondered why. Paddy Gallihan had said that Horner and his men didn't bother them up on the hill, so that couldn't be it. And Dennis himself had said that he knew Horner only by sight and reputation. But Dennis had something stuck in his craw. Every time Horner's name was mentioned, the boy became livid, then sullen. Maybe to Dennis, Horner represented someone in the Irish boy's past that Bolt couldn't know about.

He didn't have time to worry about it now. They had work to do. Maybe the anger Dennis had for Horner would work to Bolt's advantage.

"We got all Belle's cattle penned up in this one small corral, so it's just a matter of keeping your eyes peeled for anyone who thinks he can sneak in here in the dark and snag him a few head."

"Sounds easy," said Mike.

"Maybe. I want the two of you to take the first watch. From eight till midnight. Make a loop clear around the corral every so often. Keep your ears pointed good so you can hear anybody who has a mind to sneak about."

"Will do," said Dennis.

"And watch for any movement. Tom and I'll be in the bunkhouse over there." He gestured to the small building just beyond the corral. "We'll spell you about midnight."

Bolt walked over to the fire ring he and Tom had fashioned out of rocks. He pulled two sulphur matches from his pocket, struck them on a rock and touched them to the dried leaves around the logs. The flame caught immediately, spread to the kindling. Within a few minutes, the flames were licking around the logs. A breeze fanned the fire.

The four men gathered around the fire, warming their hands.

"What do you want us to do if we see one of Horner's men nosing around?" asked Mike.

"Shoot to kill," said Bolt. "They've had fair warning. From now on we play by our rules. Shoot first, ask questions later."

Bolt turned and walked toward the bunkhouse which was some twenty feet away. Tom was right on his heels, his jacket pulled tight around his neck to keep out the cold breeze. Inside, Bolt lit a coal oil lantern while Tom started a fire in the wood stove.

The bunkhouse smelled musty. It hadn't been used for a while and needed a good airing. Belle had put clean sheets and blankets on four of the bunks, dusted the shelves and table. It would do for their purpose.

"Think any troublemakers will show up tonight?" asked Tom.

"Wouldn't surprise me. Don't think Horner's men are any too bright, what I've seen of them. Did you notice how all-fired mad Dennis got when Horner's name was mentioned?"

"Yair. I reckon he could get mighty mean if he had a mind to."

"Irish temper. I hear Horner's temper is nothing to mess with."

"What are you gonna do next? Just be patient and wait him out?"

"Patience my ass. Tomorrow morning we're gonna go out and round up some stray dogies. Replenish the stock. We'll deal with Horner and his men as we need to."

****

Ferd Moss had fretted all evening. The secret he carried with him was gnawing at his gut, eating at him until he was about to explode. It wasn't his nature to keep such scandalous information to himself. Especially when it involved someone as socially prominent as Major Horner's wife.

Moss prided himself on being an extremely curious, observant person. It was his claim to fame. He considered himself a Town Crier, a hero who was capable of changing the very course of history by the truths he told to the right people. It made him feel important in the eyes of the influential men in town. It gave him a tremendous sense of power.

The Mouth. That's what they called him in town. But he didn't mind. It was better than what the kids used to call him when he was in his teens. When his body had stopped growing. All but his arms. They continued to grow like some strange appendages. That's when the younger children started calling him names. "Long Arms." "Ape boy." "Rubber

Arms." Names he detested.

As a defense against the cruelty of the other children, he became a loner, an observer of human nature. A spy, some had called him. A tattletale. But the rewards were worth the humiliation, the name calling, the loneliness. His reward came in the form of recognition. That's all he wanted.

It was after 9 p.m. when Moss scurried into the Panhandle Club. That was where most of the action was that night. That's where the men of means, the men who were more influential, gathered at night. The piano player plunked out a loud song. The music seemed to float somewhere above the din of the noisy customers. It wouldn't be long before the band came out on stage to play for the singers and dancers.

Moss found a table against the wall, as far away from the loud music as he could get. From there, he could observe the action at the bar as well as at the other tables. He glanced around the room, made a mental note of everyone in the saloon.

He noticed Luke Scarnes at the bar. Luke was talking to a couple of other men from the Rocking H. Nick Danvers and Jimmy Bill Yancy.

A thought flashed in Moss' mind.

Luke Scarnes, of course. Why hadn't he thought of him before. Luke would be the perfect one to tell his precious secret to.

Moss had fully intended to go right to Horner with the news about Elizabeth's adulterous affair. He went out to the Rocking H earlier that day to deliver the goods Elizabeth had ordered. He had even spoken to Major, but not about Elizabeth.

It was a hard thing to tell a man that his wife was

sleeping with another man. Moss knew that Horner would not take kindly to such news and Moss would lose points with the powerful man, rather than gain his favor.

Moss knew of Horner's various affairs. With that pretty little Gallihan girl and the others. But that was different. Men like Horner were not expected to remain faithful to their women. Those were things a Town Crier kept to himself. Unless they could be used to his advantage.

The decision was quick and final. Moss would tell Luke Scarnes about Horner's wife. Let Luke tell the boss. Let Luke face Horner's wrath. When the waiter came to take his drink order, Moss gave the young man a message for Scarnes.

A minute later Raymond, the youthful waiter, tapped Scarnes on the shoulder.

"The Mouth wants to know if you want to buy him a drink."

"Hell no." Scarnes glanced over at Moss.

Moss grinned, nodded his head.

Luke didn't want to buy that cheap, chisling snoop a damn thing, but he knew it was the Mouth's way of telling him that he had some information to peddle. Damn, he hated to play games with that creepy bastard.

The waiter turned to walk away. Luke's curiosity got the best of him.

"Take a couple of beers over to the Mouth's table," said Luke grudgingly as he slid off his bar stool.

"Good evening, Mr. Scarnes," said Moss, displaying a toothy grin.

"What's new?" asked Scarnes coldly.

The Mouth waited until the beers had been delivered and paid for. His head bobbed from side to side as his eyes darted around suspiciously. He hunched over, brought his long arms up on the table and looped them around in front of him.

"Cut the bullshit," barked Luke. "You got somethin' for me or not?"

"Yes, sir. I thought Mr. Horner might be interested in knowing that his wife was . . . well, to put it delicately . . . seeing another man."

Luke's eyebrows shot up.

"Elizabeth?"

"Yes, sir. Hard to believe that such a refined woman as Mrs. Horner would have a sinful affair."

"You sure?"

"I'm always sure! I seen it myself."

"Say it straight. What'd you see?"

"I saw Mrs. Horner go into the Cherokee Hotel. Didn't come back out again till almost an hour later."

"That don't prove nothin'."

"I did some checking after she left. The desk clerk clammed up tight. Wouldn't tell me anything. But one of the elderly men sitting in the lobby saw her come in and talk to a man and then go up to a room with him."

"Still don't prove nothin'."

"Yes it does. I saw the look on her face when she came out of that hotel. The look a woman gets when she's been plumbed deep."

"Who was the man?"

"Don't know that. She came out alone. The old

87

man said he'd seen the scoundrel around town but couldn't put a name to him."

"Anything else?"

"No, that's all. Just thought Horner would want to know his wife's a stray."

"All right, Moss." Scarnes got up to leave.

"Is it worth a drink of whiskey to you?" Moss groveled.

"Yeah, sure," said Luke. "I'll have one sent over." He walked back to the bar, a smirk of satisfaction on his face.

"What was that all about?" asked Nick Danvers.

"Nothing. Just bullcrap."

Luke Scarnes leaned back on his stool, pleased about what he had just learned. He despised Elizabeth Horner, the prissy bitch. She was always sticking her nose in Major's business, holding him back from his power plays. He knew that she didn't hold any love for him either.

Well, he wouldn't tell Horner just yet. But he'd keep a very close eye on Elizabeth from now on.

****

"Horner was shore riled up this mornin', wasn't he?" said Sammy Recher.

"He was just airin' the lungs," said the barrel-chested man.

Buster Burlison and the kid sat at the table in the bunkhouse at the Rocking H Ranch. The coal oil lantern in the middle of the table flickered in the small room, its scent mingling with the wood smoke from the pot bellied stove. Darkness had brought an evening chill.

In the other bunkhouse, the larger one, J. D. Walters was propped up in his bunk where he'd been all day, nursing his wounded leg. Johnny Von, his arm bandaged, sat at the table, watching five of the cowhands play poker. Some of Horner's men had gone into town to drink and carouse.

Buster Burlison poured cheap whiskey in two glasses, scooted one of them over to Sammy. The older man had already had several shots of the forty rod.

"Here, kid. Drink this. It'll put hair on your chest."

Sammy wrinkled his nose at the sharp odor of the whiskey.

"I don't take much to drinkin'."

"Drink it straight down. It's good fer ya. Calm ya down. Yer shakin' worse'n a constipated calf."

"Yeah, that was a scary experience this mornin'. I reckon I was more scared than I first thought. I ain't never been in a real shoot-out before."

"That was nothin', kid. That weren't a real gun fight. Nobody got killed."

Sammy shuddered at the thought. He took a sip of the tanglefoot. The peppery liquid burned his throat, gagged him. He coughed until his eyes watered.

"I feel mighty bad about losin' all them cattle," said Sammy when he stopped choking. "Can't really blame Horner for blowin' his stack."

"Don't pay no attention to Horner's rantings. He ain't so damned perfect. He thinks he's some kind of god, but he's got no balls." Burlison leaned back in his chair and laughed hysterically. "He's a big red-haired, red-faced galoot."

Sammy was surprised by Burlison's outburst.

"You shouldn't oughta talk about the boss that way. He'd have your hide if he heard ya."

"Well, it's true." Burlison sat up straight and downed the whiskey in his glass, poured another one. "He lost them cattle the same way he got them. By stealing. I told him I'd get the stinkin' cows back, but no, he says he don't trust me. Well, I'll show him a thing or two. I'll get those damned cattle back. By myself. Make him eat crow."

"I wouldn't do nothing hasty, Buster. 'Specially when you been drinkin'. You might not live long enough to regret it."

"Don't fret about me, boy. I kin handle my likker. I ain't no panty waste like you."

"I ain't a sissy." Sammy upended his glass, held his breath while he gulped the remainder of the whiskey. He came up coughing and sputtering, but he was satisfied that he had proved his point. The whiskey burned his throat, hit his gut like a lead ball. He was immediately sick to his stomach. When he tried to stand up, his legs became rubbery spindles. He was dizzy, disoriented. He ran outside the bunkhouse where he heaved until he thought his guts would turn inside out. The foul-tasting bile scratched his throat. He stood outside for a few moments breathing in the cold night air, trying to regain his composure.

Pale and weak, he finally walked back into the bunkhouse. He didn't look at Burlison, but went straight to his cot.

"I'm goin' to bed," he mumbled.

The older man's laughter roared in his ears, grated against his shattered nerves.

"Don't worry, kid, you'll learn to drink when you grow up. You just give up too easy. Not me." Buster pounded his chest with his fist. "I don't give up on nothin'. I'll get them cattle back. You wait and see."

Sammy didn't want to hear any more of Burlison's drunken talk. He crawled into his bunk, turned his back to the barrel-chested man, pulled the covers up around his neck. He lay perfectly still, trying to settle his stomach down. He hoped he wouldn't have to make another run for the outside.

Buster Burlison ran his fingers through his thick, bristly beard. He wasn't laughing anymore. He was thinking about the humiliation he had suffered. Twice that same day, he had been made to feel like a fool. First when Bolt and his partner had outsmarted them and stolen the cattle right out from under their noses. And then later, when Horner had given him and Sammy and J. D. a tongue lashing in front of all the other cowhands. Only Johnny Von had escaped Horner's wrath. That was because Johnny wasn't afraid of no man, not even Horner.

Hornet. That would be a better name for Major Horner. He had certainly been mad that morning. Mad as a wet hornet. Buster smiled when he thought about the giant man pacing the floor, ranting and raving like a crazy man, his face turning as red as his hair. It's a wonder he didn't pop a blood vessel.

He didn't like to admit it, even to himself, but Buster knew that Johnny had been right about that morning. Bolt and his friend could easily have killed all four of them. Even if Sammy hadn't been such a bumbling idiot, Bolt could have nailed them.

Resentments began to boil up in Burlison. He hated Johnny Von for being so damned calm when faced with Horner's rage. And yet, he respected him for it. He loathed Bolt, the sneaky bastard.

Well, he'd show Horner who the best man was. Who the bravest man was. He'd go out there tonight and get all them cows back.

He was just drunk enough to try it.

CHAPTER NINE

Bolt hadn't been able to sleep. It had been quiet while the Gallihan boys were taking the first watch. Almost too quiet.

The wind had come up strong in the last couple of hours and more than once Bolt was startled by the noise of branches tapping on the bunkhouse windows. He was keyed up, edgy, like a hair trigger ready to go off at the slightest provocation. The wind always did that to him, made him uneasy.

But it was more than that, he knew. His hunches were almost always right. And tonight he had a gut feeling that there would be trouble. He could smell it in the air, feel it in his bones.

Bolt walked over to the bunk in the corner, shook Tom awake.

"Rise and shine, cowboy. Time to earn your keep."

"Who . . . wha . . . oh shit, I was deep under." Tom sat up, threw the covers back. He swung his legs over the edge of the cot. Just as he reached for his boots, the wind forced a tree branch to scratch at the window.

Tom jumped up, reached for his pistol which he

had stashed under his pillow.

"You come up fighting, don't you," Bolt chided. "It's just the wind. Come on, it should be about midnight. Time to spell the boys. They must be near frozen. That wind is fierce."

Outside, the young cousins stood over the fire, warming their hands. They had just finished riding around the corral in opposite directions, passing each other half way around. The only noice they had heard all evening was the muffled yapping of distant coyotes. The wind rustling through the tree leaves sounded like a rushing river.

"Sure wish that wind would die down," said Dennis.

"Yeah, it's spooky out here. I keep hearing things that aren't there." Mike stared down at the fire, hypnotized by the flames lapping at the logs.

Dennis heard a noise. He froze in position, cocked his head, strained to hear.

"Listen," he whispered. "I hear something."

"The wind," said Mike, not taking his eyes off the flames.

"No. Something metal. Over by the corral, I think." He heard the soft clanking again. "Someone's trying to open the gate." His voice was a whisper. "Wait here. I'm going to check it out."

Dennis drew his pistol, crouched low. Quickly, he ran for the corral gate, keeping his profile low, his steps light.

Buster Burlison saw the dark form approaching just as he stepped into the pen. It was coming up fast. He started back out the gate, but it was too late. The shadowy figure was already at the gate, slamming it shut. Buster looked around, could see very little in the dark. He made a run for it. Right through the cattle in the pen.

From outside the corral, Dennis aimed his pistol at the intruder. He knew he couldn't get a clean shot. Too many cows in there.

The cattle started moving around, bawling at the confusion.

Dennis ran around the outside of the fence, saw the big man jumping the fence a short distance from where the fire burned.

"Get him, Mike," Dennis yelled. "He's on your side."

"Cows sound restless," Tom was saying when they heard Dennis shout.

"What the hell . . ." said Bolt, dashing to the bunkhouse door.

Mike looked up, tried to pick out the escaping man. He couldn't see anything. The light of the fire had temporarily blinded him. He blinked, couldn't get rid of the bright spots that lingered before his eyes. He blinked again, thought he saw a shadow. He fired at it. The bullet thunked into a log in the tall woodpile. He heard the footsteps now, two sets of them, running in different directions. He couldn't shoot again. He knew one of the men running was Dennis. He couldn't see enough to tell which one.

Dennis came around the end of the fence just as Burlison crossed near the fire and headed for the open field behind the corral. Burlison fired a wild shot on the run.

Dennis took aim, squeezed the trigger. He heard the cattle thief cry out, crash to the ground.

Cautiously, Dennis closed in on the fallen man. The crumpled body sprawled on the ground a few feet from the glowing fire, motionless.

Bolt ran up, his pistol drawn. Penrod was right behind him.

"Who is it?" Bolt asked when he saw the bloody body glistening in the fireglow.

"Don't know," said Dennis. "You said to shoot first, ask questions later. He was trying to steal the cattle."

Bolt leaned down and pushed the body over so he could see the face of the mangled man.

"One of Horner's men, all right," Bolt said. "I've seen him. They called him Buster."

"Wish it had been Horner," Dennis mumbled.

"How'd it happen?"

Dennis told him.

"I couldn't see him," Mike said. "Couldn't see a damned thing. I was watching the fire right before it happened and when I looked up, it was like I was blind."

"The guy must have been crazy to try a stunt like this by himself," said Dennis.

"Or drunk," said Tom. "He reeks of forty rod."

Bolt stroked his stubbled chin, turned to Mike.

"You learned something mighty important to-night, Mike. Any time you got reason to be out at night, you got reason to be careful. Never look at a fire direct, or any light for that matter. It'll blind you just as sure as somebody poked both eyes out with a stick. Could cost you your skin, somebody sneaks up on you."

"Don't worry," said Mike. "It won't ever happen again."

"This man have a horse?" Bolt asked Dennis.

"Yeah. I saw one out by the gate."

"See if you two can catch it up. We'll send Buster back home, toes down."

✱✱✱✱✱✱✱

Major Horner woke up in a foul mood. He hadn't slept well the night before. The howling wind kept him awake and he had spent a good part of the night fuming over the fact that he hadn't been able to buy Bolt off. Something had to be done. Soon.

He wanted that VeeBee land in the worst way. He was used to getting what he wanted. Bolt was the hangup, clear and simple. He knew that. If Bolt hadn't come along and stuck his nose in, it would be a different story. He'd have that land by now, lock, stock and barrel. Belle and Ginny would have been forced out by now if it weren't for that bastard Bolt.

The giant man got out of bed, stretched his arms over his head and yawned. The early morning light filtered through the thin curtains, changing the objects in the room from black to gray and finally to soft natural pastels.

Horner glanced down at his wife who was still sleeping. She looked beautiful, like an ancient fair-haired goddess waiting for a handsome prince to come along and kiss her awake.

Horner wondered why she had acted so strangely last evening. Usually Elizabeth was warm, enthusiastic about life, joyful as she bustled about. But last night had been different. During supper she had been quiet, sullen. Later, when he asked her what was wrong, she became defensive, insolent. She retired early, excusing herself by saying she was tired. Maybe she was ill and didn't want to bother him about it. It would be like her to do that.

Horner slipped into his heavy wool robe, walked over to the window, pulled the curtain back. He did this every morning, rain or shine. He liked to look over the expanse of land he owned every morning. It was a good way to start the day.

The wind was gone. The sun would be up in a few minutes. The layer of clouds he could see from the window were turning pink, shades of salmon and orange. It would be a good day.

As he scanned the landscape, something caught his eye.

A dark shape in the middle of the field that he had never noticed before. He knew it couldn't be a tree unless it had sprouted overnight. As the sky lightened a bit, he thought the figure looked like a fully loaded pack mule. He strained his eyes until they blurred trying to figure out what the strange form was.

The sky brightened and he saw that it was a horse. With a saddle on it, he thought. Probably one of his men up early, ready to ride out to do some work. He turned around, started to walk away from the window.

Something made him look again.

There was a man strapped to that horse. Dead, or

bad hurt.

Horner dressed in a hurry. He went out the back door, walked through the field the hundred yards or so to the horse. He knew who the man was before he reached him. Only one man was that big: Buster Burlison.

Flies swarmed over the body, buzzed around the gaping hole in Burlison's back. The stench of death soured Major's stomach.

A half hour later, Horner had questioned all his men. Only the kid, Sammy Recher, could offer a clue.

"He was goin' on about how he was gonna get all them cows back. Said he'd do it by himself, make you eat crow. I thought it was just drunk talk. I didn't think he'd really try it. Honest I didn't."

Horner's face turned red.

"Thanks, Sammy. Luke, I want to talk to you," he said, dismissing the others.

He waited until they were in his study before he exploded.

"Damn it, Luke. Enough is enough! How many more men do I have to lose before this is over? I want Bolt stopped! Out of the way! What about that man you sent for?"

"He should be on his way by now."

"We gotta do something."

Horner paced across the room, came back and sat on the edge of his desk. He ran his fingers through his thick red hair.

"Bolt's an outlaw, right?"

"Right."

"There's got to be a wanted poster out on him,"

said Major.

"Right again. I've heard there's one over at the sheriff's office. Think it's the only one in town."

"Then not everyone in these parts knows he's wanted."

"I don't get your point."

"I want every man, woman and child in this territory to know that Bolt's a criminal, a dangerous outlaw wanted for murder and bank robbery."

"How you gonna do that?" asked the scar-faced man.

"I want enough posters to plaster them all over town. We'll put them in every shop window, in every saloon, every whorehouse. We'll even tack one to the door of the church if we need to. We'll stick 'em on every fence post, every bare space we can find." Horner's eyes glittered with a crazy light. "Nail them to anything that doesn't move. Somebody will see them and need the money. He'll have so many people after him, someone will do the job."

"Now wait a minute," Scarnes interjected. "Just slow down, Major. How are you gonna get that many posters?"

"Find out where they came from and order some."

"That would take too long."

"Find someone to print us some new ones. Maybe talk to the sheriff. He'll know how to get the posters."

"How many do you want?"

"Fifty ought to do it."

"There ain't that many places to put them," objected Luke.

"We'll find places, even if I have to shove one up

your ass."

****

The wind blew itself out during the night and it was bright and calm when Bolt woke up after two hours sleep. It was shortly after eight o'clock when he sent the Gallihan boys home. He told them to have Paddy come over in about an hour.

"You gonna have Paddy stand watch?" Tom asked after breakfast.

"No. No need to guard the cattle during the day. We'll be working around here anyway. He can help us with the branding."

As they walked outside, Tom turned to Bolt.

"Think Horner knows about last night yet? That is, if the horse made it back home with the fat man's body."

"My guess is that Horner knows. A horse will always head for home if he's got nobody to tell him otherwise."

"True," said Tom. "Horner knows. What do you think he'll do?"

"Don't much matter. I'm not going to sit around waiting for his reaction. It's going to be a busy day. A busy week. It's time to replace the VeeBee stock. We're going to go in and grab up every stray cow we can find. We'll start out on the far corners of Horner's land. It'll take some doing, some hard work."

"Yair."

"There's a lot more to do than round up strays. We'll need bigger pens right away. By nightfall, I

101

plan to double the count."

Tom's eyebrows shot up.

"You mean you're actually going to go on Horner's land and steal his cattle? That's rustling. It's against the law you know."

"Fuck the law."

"Kinda dangerous territory right now, don't you think?"

"Nobody said life would be easy. Get the branding irons ready."

CHAPTER TEN

The three men worked fast and furious all morning. By noon Bolt had rounded up thirty strays from a far corner of the Rocking H. None of them carried brands.

At the ranch, Penrod and Paddy Gallihan kept the iron hot, branding all the strays as quick as Bolt delivered them. They also branded the cattle that were already in the fenced pasture.

"Lunch is ready, boys," Belle announced when she walked out to the pasture. She was dressed in a long gingham dress. The bib apron she wore over it didn't conceal her hourglass figure.

"Is it that time already?" said Bolt. "I didn't even know you were home yet."

"We got here about an hour ago." She looked at Bolt and grinned. His face was smudged with dirt. "Wash your face before you come to dinner," she said as she turned away.

"I'll wash my whole body if you'll do the scrubbing," Bolt called.

"Don't tempt me," she laughed and then ran to the house.

The three men washed as much dirt as they could off their hands and faces before they went into the house. The aroma of cooking food filled their nostrils when they stepped inside.

"Sit down," said Belle. "Any place you like."

Five places were set at the table. Steam rose from the blue platter that held a big pot roast. It was in the middle of the table. Two large bowls held hot boiled potatoes and browned gravy. Smaller bowls offered homemade strawberry jam and watermelon pickles. Fresh churned butter was at one end of the table.

Ginny entered the dining room, a bowl of steaming green beans in one hand, a basket of muffins in the other.

"Good afternoon," she said. "Hope you men are hungry."

"Starved," said Tom.

"You gals outdid yourselves," smiled Bolt when he saw the spread of food.

"It's the least we can do," said Belle. "You're all doing so much for us."

Bolt looked up at Ginny. She turned away when their eyes met. It was deliberate, he was sure. He wondered why. It was almost as if she was afraid of him. More likely she was just cold toward men, like Belle said. She gave the impression that she thought she was better than anyone else. She always had that little nose of hers stuck up so high in the air, it was a wonder it didn't catch flies. Bolt didn't cotton much to a woman who acted so prissy.

He tried to keep his eyes off her, but they automatically swung back to her, as if drawn by a strong magnetic force. He felt a quiver in the pit of his stomach; a warmth that coursed through his veins. Damned if she wasn't some handsome; a fine-looking woman. His hunger was not confined to the vittles.

Bolt wasn't the only one who noticed Ginny's stark beauty. Tom and Penrod gave her the once-over, as well. She looked absolutely ravishing, even in her ranch clothes which consisted of blue denims and a plaid shirt that was designed for a man. She hadn't bothered to button the top two buttons and she wore no bra under the shirt. Her dark silken hair was pulled back from her face, tied in back with a bow.

She set the food on the table, felt Bolt's eyes boring into her.

"I'll get the coffee," she said. For an instant, she glared at Bolt with deep blue eyes. It was a look that said, "Hands off, mister."

Bolt had to stifle a laugh. She needn't worry. He wasn't a woman chaser and he wasn't interested in a cold fish.

Bolt realized how hungry he was when he started eating. He managed to keep his mind and eyes off Ginny during most of the meal. Only once did the quiver return to the pit of his stomach. It was when she got up to get more coffee. He couldn't help looking at her long legs in those tight jeans.

"Thanks for the good meal, girls," Bolt said when he could eat no more.

"Our pleasure," said Belle as she started to clear away the dishes.

"I think I'll get a couple hours sleep. It may be another long night. You can go on home, Paddy. Won't be needing you any more today. You can help with the branding again tomorrow, if that's all right."

"Fine with me."

"Tom, you tired?" Bolt asked.

"Hell no. I got my eight hours beauty sleep."

"We're going to need another roll or two of that Glidden wire to patch the fence so we can turn the cattle out to pasture. Feel like taking the wagon in to town and getting it?"

"Sure. Got nothing better to do."

Bolt detected a note of sarcasm in Tom's words.

"Don't get lost. I aim to scare up a few more head before dark takes over."

"Do you want to sleep in the back bedroom, Bolt?" Belle asked. "It'll be quiet there."

"No. I'll sleep out in the bunkhouse where I won't bother anybody." It was a cutting remark and he stared right at Ginny when he said it. It was his way of letting her know that he didn't plan to rape her right there in broad daylight in front of God and everybody. It was his way of telling her that he wasn't the least bit interested in her body.

But he was interested.

He thought about her as he stripped down to his shorts and climbed in the bunk. He thought about her rare beauty, her long graceful legs, as he pulled the sheet over him.

He didn't think about her very long.

He fell asleep the minute his head hit the pillow.

****

His dreams were full of green pastures and dark

106

creatures who were half man, half beast.

From somewhere deep down in his sleep filled mind, he sensed a warmth at his crotch.

He dreamed of dark stallions with long slender legs.

He struggled to pull his conscious mind up out of the deep fog of sleep.

Some small corner of his consciousness felt the warm bare skin touching his own.

"Long . . . legs . . . Ginn . . . y . . ." His words were broken, barely audible, like ice turning to slush.

His consciousness floated to the top.

He woke with a start. This was no dream. The smooth bare flesh seared against his. A warm thigh pressed against his leg. Inside his shorts, a sensuous hand groped for his manhood. The erection had already begun. His eyes fluttered open.

"Belle?"

"Who'd you expect?" Belle was stark naked.

He pulled her close, kissed her passionately. She squeezed his mass of flesh, felt it grow in her hand.

"You don't need these," she said, pushing his shorts down. He helped her by bringing his knees up while she slid his shorts down past his ankles. She left them where they fell, a small lump at the foot of the bed.

She sprawled on top of him, her body light as a down comforter. She squirmed around until the portal to her sex was resting against his erection. Her spongy breasts crushed against his chest.

Bolt stretched his body taut beneath her, then relaxed to enjoy her eager manipulations. She bent her head down and kissed him with a fervent passion.

Her tongue slid inside his mouth, searched out his tongue. Her body became an undulating form above him, a sea of passion gently splashing over his wakened senses. She rolled around, her sex cleft rubbing against his throbbing organ.

"Want to sit on the peg?" Bolt husked.

Without answering, Belle sat up straight on his lap, moved enough to position herself directly over his rigid organ. With one hand, she guided the shaft to her pussy. She slid down, swallowing the stiff pole with eager, slippery lips.

Bolt gasped as he felt her damp sheath clamp down on his cock. He lifted his head off the pillow and looked down. He could see her dark thatch envelop his swollen cock as she rocked up and down. He lowered his head to the pillow again and watched her face. It was a study of pure passion. There wasn't a painter alive who could capture her expression.

He grabbed her buttocks with firm hands, pulled her down on him, held her there tightly. He thrust his hips upward, matched her rhythm. He watched the expression on her face change from passion to relief as her eyes glazed over. She held her breath, felt that one brief second of ecstasy that comes with orgasm. He held her close to him, felt her pussy spasm and become damper.

"Let me on top." His voice was raspy, sensuous.

"Oh, yes. I want you to do it to me."

She started to climb off, but instead slid up, across his chest, until she straddled his shoulders. Her pussy was right in his face. He kissed her sensitive, secret places, ran his tongue around the folds of her sheath.

A moment later she bucked with pleasure, clamped her knees against his ears as she had another orgasm.

Bolt rolled her over on her back, slid easily into her well-oiled pussy. He stroked her slow and deep, surprised that she was still so tight. She excited him so much that he knew he was about to explode. He varied his stroking, holding back his intense desires. He withdrew his spear, pushed the head of it back inside the warm sheath. His cock went in slowly, deliberately, until he had thrust it to the hilt.

She wriggled her hips beneath him, encouraging him to give her more. He pumped her slow and easy, staying himself as long as he could. He wanted it to last forever, it was so good. Gradually, his stroking became faster, deeper, until it was too late.

He felt his seed begin to boil, surface to the tip of his mushroom head, spurt out, splashing against the walls of her womb. He grunted and groaned like a crazed animal. He plunged in deep, stayed there until the throbbing had subsided.

Finally, when his organ went limp, he rolled off of her. He snuggled up close to her warm body, leaned his head back on the pillow. He stared at the ceiling.

"That was good, Belle. You're good. Thanks."

"It was good for me, too."

She got up, started to dress.

"I've got to get back over to the house," she said.

"I should get to work, too."

She dressed quickly. She walked to the door, then turned around and walked back over close to Bolt. He had his trousers on and was sitting on the edge of the bed putting his shirt on.

"Bolt?"

"Yeah?" He looked up, saw that her face was serious.

"Who were you thinking of?"

"What?"

"Who were you thinking of when we . . . when we did it?"

"What in the hell are you talking about?"

"When I first came in here . . . well, you said something about long legs. And I thought you called Ginny's name. Would make sense. Ginny's the one with long legs. Not me. You were thinking about her like you did before." Her old jealousy had cropped up again.

"Oh, for crissakes, woman. You gonna start that again? I was sound asleep when you came in here with your hot little body. You woke me up. I wasn't thinking of anything. Of anybody! You always have to spoil a good thing by attacking me afterwards!"

She backed off.

"I'm sorry, Bolt. I just thought . . ."

"Don't think."

"Bolt, don't. I was wrong, I know. I don't want to fight with you. You're right. I thought I wasn't jealous anymore. But I am! Of you, dammit!"

"You bring it on yourself, you know. There was a saying my father used to preach to his congregation. It's from Job. It went something like, 'That which I fear the most has come upon me.' That's the way I feel. I remember this one man who came to my father for help. The man always complained about his lot in life and finally lost everything he had, his home, his ranch, his family, his pride. My father told him he had created his own fate by thinking only bad things were going to happen to him.

"It's the same with you, Belle. If you keep thinking the worst of everyone, that's the way they'll react to you. Think good things about yourself and you'll feel better. Do you know what I'm trying to say?"

"Yes, I do, but it's easier said than done."

"It's simple, Belle. Let me give you another Bible quotation. My father ended every sermon with this one. It's from Mark 11:24. 'What things soever ye desire, when ye pray, believe that ye receive them, and ye shall have them.' That's the way I believe. Enjoy life without attaching strings to everything. Do what pleases you, whatever you're comfortable with. Believe things will be good and you'll make a happy life for yourself."

"Is that what you do, Bolt? You always seem to be so . . . so damned sure of yourself."

"Now you know my secret," he grinned.

"You know something. I really like you, Bolt. As a person. You're your own man and I admire that. You're a very special person."

"Thank you, Belle. You're special yourself."

"Hey, I've really got to get back to the house. See you later."

"Belle," he said seriously as she turned away, "there's just one more thing."

"What's that?" Her eyes searched him for a clue.

"As long as I've got a face, you've got a place to sit." He broke up with laughter.

"Oh, you . . . you louse," she grinned. She leaned

over and picked up one of his boots, hurled it at him.

He grabbed the covers and pulled them around his head.

Just in time.

****

Ginny saw Belle sneak out to the bunkhouse.

She knew what was going on out there. She was disgusted that Belle would throw herself at a man like that. Even a man as sexy as Bolt.

Not that she was a prude because she wasn't. She'd had her share of men when she was in her teens. She just didn't like the way they treated women. Not after what she'd been through with her husband.

She thought about Belle and Bolt in the bunkhouse.

She wondered what kind of a lover Bolt was.

CHAPTER ELEVEN

"Something's wrong," said Bolt. "Been too quiet around here the past week."

"I reckon Horner's given up," said Tom Penrod. "A man knows when he's beat."

"Horner's not the type to give up so easy. No, he's got something up his sleeve."

"He's had enough time to make a move if he was going to, Jared. Nothing's happened. I thought he'd come after us when he saw that fat man Buster come back strapped on his horse with his lamp blowed out. And I can't believe we scared up so many cows from over there without him batting an eye. We got more than five hundred of them and I know some of his boys saw us. It's almost like he told his hands to let us have whatever we wanted."

"You believe that, Tom?"

"Well, I think he's got a yeller streak down his back a foot wide."

"Don't be so sure. Horner doesn't want to dirty his hands. He wants some flunky to do his coolie work for him. Man like that is greedy. He won't stop until he's got everything he wants. Won't stop then because no matter how much he gets, he'll still want more."

"Well, if it stays this quiet," said Tom, "I'd sure like to take a night off. We haven't been guarding at night anyway the past couple of nights."

"Why don't you say it straight," Bolt grinned. "You're horny."

"Think you could handle it tonight if I stay in town, tend to some business?"

"Business? You just want to get laid. Yeah, go ahead. I see you straining at your halter, Tom. We need a break in the routine. I'm getting itchy myself. Think I'll head in to town too, see what's going on. Maybe find a good poker game this afternoon."

****

It was mid-afternoon when Bolt saddled his horse, Nick, and headed for town. Tom rode with him.

Bolt got his first smell of trouble before he reached the main street.

He saw the poster tacked to the big oak tree at the edge of town. He eased his horse over for a closer look.

"REWARD — $2000 — JARED BOLT — Wanted dead or alive. For murder and bank robbery. Signed, Judge Andrew Jackson Wilkins, Fort Scott, Kansas Territory."

A drawing of Bolt's face was centered on the flyer. Black ink stood out against the stark white paper. Bolt ran a thumb across the ink. The ink smeared.

"This hasn't been printed too long ago," said Bolt. "The ink's still wet."

114

"Think this is Horner's doing?" asked Tom.

"I'm sure of it."

"Mighty big poster, ain't it?"

"Twice as big as the original flyer out on me. Pretty good likeness of me, don't you think?"

"Ugly as sin," Tom grinned.

Bolt ripped the poster from the tree, folded it and jammed it in his jacket pocket. He removed a plug of Levi Garrett chewing tobacco, tore off a chunk with his teeth, stuffed it in his mouth.

"Make a nice souvenir." He pulled the reins to the left, got Nick back on the road.

Bolt rode on in to town.

The hackles rose on the back of his neck when he reached the main street. He pulled back on the reins. The sight gave him an eerie feeling. Plastered to every building, every post, every false front in town were more posters. Everywhere he looked, he saw the same large, glaring posters.

"Horner doesn't have to hire no gunnies," Bolt said wryly. "Lot of poor folk here could use two thousand bucks."

"Let's hope not."

"There'll be those who'll try it."

"You aim to light a shuck?"

"Hell no. At least I know where I stand. I came to town to play poker and that's just what I aim to do."

"Step lightly and keep your shooting hand free," Tom warned.

"Always do."

"See you later. Don't be surprised if I don't get back to the ranch till morning."

"Nothing you'd do would surprise me."

115

Tom rode on to the Cimarron Hotel. He planned to take a nice long bath before he sought out the pleasures of one of the local glitter gals.

Bolt rode directly to the Brass Rail Saloon. That's where the good poker games were, he'd heard. He dismounted, tied Nick to the hitchrail in front of the saloon. He glanced at the wanted poster fastened to the post near his horse. He spit a stream of brown tobacco juice at the flyer. A glob of it hit the center of the poster, ran down the paper to form ugly brown stains.

The boards creaked under his boots as he walked along the boardwalk to the batwing doors.

Another poster. Tacked on the door. He swung the doors open, walked inside, his hand hovering at his side. If anyone was going to take a pot shot at him, this would be a good place to do it.

He made a quick assessment, walked to the bar. Men looked up, eyed him suspiciously. He ordered a beer from the bartender, noticed another poster. This one, hung hastily, partially covered a whiskey ad. He sensed the hostility when the bartender served his drink.

He carried the beer to a table near the back of the room where he could watch the poker game, wait for an opening.

Six men sat at the round table. The one facing Bolt was low on chips. It wouldn't be a long wait.

Bolt studied the players, watched for telltale movements they made when they had the good hands. The man who was losing was a hardcase, a drifter, Bolt figured. The others called him Charley. He had mean, cold eyes that became slits when he

116

drew the bad cards. Charley was dealt five cards. He discarded two of them, tapped on the table for two new ones. His brown eyes became slits and he folded before the bidding got going. He glanced up, saw Bolt watching him.

Another man at the table drew Bolt's attention.

He was one of Horner's men. Johnny Von. Bolt had tangled with him before. Had winged him, in fact, when Bolt caught him trespassing on the VeeBee Ranch with Buster Burlison and the kid and another Rocking H hand. That had been more than a week ago.

Von seemed to be the big winner at the moment. He had chips stacked in front of him four inches deep.

Once, between deals, Johnny Von stretched his arms, glanced over his shoulder. He saw Bolt. His expression never changed.

It took Bolt a while to detect Von's body quirks when he got the good cards, but he finally spotted it. Every time Von brought his cards up and touched his chin with the top of his cards, as if to conceal his cards from the others, he raked in the pot.

Charley's chips dwindled. It was no wonder. He wasn't concentrating on the game. He spent more time staring at Bolt than a man should when he's playing for big stakes.

Charley threw in all his chips on a wild bet. He hadn't squinted his eyes. He had a good hand. Two pair. Aces over kings.

Von beat him with a full house.

"That does it for me." Charley got up, leaving an empty chair.

Bolt rose from his seat, took a few steps toward the poker table.

Charley walked by Bolt, deliberately brushed against him.

Bolt looked up, found himself staring into the man's cold eyes.

"Your name Bolt?" Charley asked.

The men at the poker table looked up.

"You got it right."

Charley's eyes became tiny slits. His lips curled to a snarl. His hand flew to his holster. His pistol cleared leather in the bat of an eye. It was already cocked by the time it was waist high. He squeezed the trigger as he raised the gun. It was aimed point blank at Bolt's chest.

Bolt's gun was quicker. He saw it coming, side stepped as his hand streaked to his Colt. He thumbed back on the hammer as he brought it up, fired a half second later.

Charley's shot missed Bolt, crashed into the mirror behind the bar, a few inches from the wanted poster. Men sitting at the bar jumped, began to scatter.

At the same instant, Bolt's bullet caught Charley in the heart. He moaned once, was dead before he hit the floor. Blood spurted out of the gaping hole in his chest. There was a small neat hole in the man's shirt where the bullet ripped through it. A pool of blood began to form under the body, spread until the man's head was face down in the sticky fluid.

Charley was the first one to try it. Bolt knew there would be others who would take up the challenge offered by the new posters in town. He would be ready for them.

He glanced around the room, knew that every man in the saloon had seen the posters. They couldn't have missed them.

"Gentlemen," said Bolt. "May I join your game?"

Johnny Von stared at Bolt, said nothing. The other four men looked at each other, waiting for someone to give Bolt an answer.

Finally, an older, distinguished-looking man with a healthy stack of chips in front of him nodded to Bolt to sit down in the empty chair.

"You got the money, we got the time," said the gray-haired man. A cigar dangled from his thick lips. "The name's Robert Markey." He didn't offer his hand.

Bolt slipped into the empty chair, to Markey's left. Johnny Von sat directly opposite Bolt. It was Markey's deal. He shuffled the cards, offered the deck to Bolt.

"Slice the deck?"

Bolt cut the deck thin, pushed it back to Markey.

The man on the other side of Bolt looked down at Charley's bloody body sprawled on the floor. He gave Bolt a hard look, then stood up and excused himself.

"I've had enough for now," he said.

The gambler sitting on the other side of Markey followed suit. He pushed his chair away from the table.

"Me too. Thanks for the game." He scooped his chips up and stuffed them in his pocket. That left four players.

The game went fast with Markey winning the hand. The players paid little attention to the removal of the dead man. Three men carried him outside and to the undertaker's.

Bolt raked in the next pot and Von caught the next two.

Two more hands and the fourth man, Eddie, cashed in his chips.

Bolt watched the two remaining gamblers, did his bidding according to the body quirks they displayed. When Von touched his cards to his chin, Bolt held back. When Markey set his cigar in the ash tray and sat up straight, Bolt knew he was concentrating on a good hand.

Bolt lost a few, won a few, but gradually he was taking in more chips than he was giving out. Markey's stack grew shorter.

"Think I'll bow out while I still got my skin," said Markey. "Let you two battle it out. I'd like to sit a spell and watch you, if that's all right."

Bolt nodded.

The competition became fierce. Von spoke only when he had to, but he glared at Bolt with an unnerving steely gaze.

Von looked at his hand, tapped his chin with the cards. He looked like he was contemplating his next bid, but Bolt knew Von had drawn a good hand.

Bolt bet his own hand. His cards were good enough he figured he could beat Von. The bidding put five hundred dollars in the pot. Bolt's hand was better. Straight flush to a straight.

Bolt won the pot.

Von glared at him as Bolt dragged the chips from the middle of the table. As Bolt shuffled the deck, Von rubbed his upper arm as if to remind Bolt that he hadn't forgotten that Bolt had shot him in that arm.

Bolt read the message. Loud and clear.

As the game progressed, each man held his own. Few men could beat Bolt at poker, but Von managed to rake in his share of the pots. The bids got higher. The pots got sweeter.

After almost two hours of playing, they still managed to stay on an even keel.

It was Von's deal.

He called the game: five card draw.

Bolt waited until all the cards were dealt before he picked them up. He discarded three cards, kept a king and jack of hearts. He tapped on the table for three more cards.

Von needed two cards. He held three aces. Diamonds, spades and clubs.

Bolt looked at the new cards. He couldn't have been luckier.

Von gathered up his cards, fanned them out to fit his hand. His expression remained the same. Slowly, he brought the cards up to his chin, let them rest there a minute. He had drawn two kings. He glared at Bolt, waited for Bolt's bid.

Bolt played it cool, raised only a small amount the first time around. Von raised five hundred. Bolt matched him, raised another five hundred.

Von held the cards to his chin, sure of his hand.

"Match you and raise you a thousand." Von pushed all his chips to the center of the table.

Bolt wrapped his fingers around his stack of chips, lifted them up and let ten chips clank to the table. He shoved them into the pot.

"I'll see you."

Johnny Von proudly turned over the fanned cards. He had a full house. He reached for the pot.

"Not so fast," said Bolt. He spread his cards out in front of him. He had a royal flush in hearts.

Von drew his hand back like it had been burned by a hot poker.

"Shit!" said Von. The anger showed on his face. He pushed his chair back and stood up. He reached for his shirt pocket.

The sudden movement set Bolt's adrenalin flowing. Bolt's hand shot to his side. His hand hovered above his holster.

Von stuck his hand into the pocket, drew out the makings for a cigarette. Casually, he rolled a quirly, offered Bolt the makings. It was hard for Von not to laugh at Bolt's reaction. If he had been going for his gun, Bolt would have nailed him.

"You play a damn fine game," Von said, extending his hand. Bolt shook it and then accepted the tobacco and papers.

"So do you," said Bolt.

"I'd like to play you again some time soon." Johnny Von had a new respect for Bolt. He knew that Bolt played an honest game. He also knew that Bolt was quick, always ready and that Bolt wouldn't take any guff off of anybody.

"I'd like that," said Bolt. He scooped the chips into his hat, went to cash them in.

The sun was low in the sky when Bolt stepped outside the saloon.

He knew someone was waiting for him.

His hand hovered above his holster as he whirled around to his left.

CHAPTER TWELVE

Bolt had seen the movement out of the corner of his eye. He saw it the instant he walked out of the saloon, through the batwing doors. A blur as someone darted behind the building.

He stepped back against the building, drawing his pistol in the same movement. He pressed himself against the wall, turned his head to the left. He waited, his pistol cocked.

He stood absolutely motionless, calm on the outside. But inside his guts were churning. His nerves jangled like a hundred cowbells at milking time. His breath was slow, measured.

The man stuck his head around the corner, stepped out.

Bolt's gun was hot and fast. He blasted the man in the face. The impact rocked him backwards. He slumped to the ground, his face blown away.

Bolt heard footsteps behind him.

He whirled around, shot again.

He dropped the man who had a Colt aimed at him. Dead in his tracks. The bullet caught the gunnie in the throat, tore out his voice box. The man tried to scream. Nothing came out but blood.

The townspeople ran in all directions. Most of them sought the cover of the buildings. They ducked into stores or saloons. Whatever was handy. Some ducked behind the water trough. Others hid behind the horses tied to the hitchrails.

Bolt held back, waiting to see if he would be challenged again.

Johnny Von came out of the Brass Rail to see what was happening. He saw Bolt's pistol still smoking. He looked around, saw the two dead men on the ground.

Bolt expected Von to draw. He didn't.

The main street was deathly silent. No one moved.

Finally, Bolt reloaded and holstered his pistol. He moved away from the building. It was like a signal to the people that the fireworks were over.

The townspeople came out of their hiding places, began to mill around, talk about the fast gun, the dead men. Women peered out of store windows, afraid to come out on the street.

Bolt eyed Von suspiciously.

Von's hand floated above his holster. His face was noncommittal, a poker face.

The suspense ate at Bolt's guts. He wished Von would make his move if he was going to.

Bolt turned his back on Von, walked slowly away from him. He felt the hackles on the back of his neck rise. It was a bad thing to turn your back on a man you didn't trust. It took more guts to turn and walk away than it did to stand there waiting.

The boards creaked under his weight. His ear was attuned to every noise behind him. He kept expecting

124

the bullet in the back. His eyes searched the crowd in front of him, watching for any sudden movement.

Bolt reached his horse. He turned so he was facing Von, his back to the crowd. He noticed that Von hadn't drawn his gun. He let out a breath, began untying Nick.

When Bolt turned to face the saloon, three men jumped out from behind the water trough. Bolt's back was to them. They dashed toward Bolt, pistols in their hands.

"Behind you, Bolt!"

The warning came from Johnny Von.

Bolt whipped around, saw the blur of the three men bracing him. His pistol cleared leather quicker than before. He shot two of them before they could fire. One of them took a chest shot. The other caught it in the head when Bolt's pistol bucked.

The third man was on top of him.

Bolt swung to fire, wasn't quick enough.

The gunman squeezed the trigger.

Too late.

A bullet crashed into the third man, knocking him backwards, to his death.

Bolt hadn't fired the bullet. He looked around, saw Von's pistol smoking.

Bolt stood there a moment, watching the dying men writhing on the ground. The shots were fatal, he knew. The townsmen clustered around the wounded men to see how bad they were.

The yammer of voices jabbed at Bolt's ear.

"Go get the doctor!" yelled one of them.

"Too late. Get the undertaker," hollered another.

"Get the sheriff over here!"

"Fast gun."

"That's Bolt!"

"I seen him kill a man before. I mean he's fast!"

"The bounty money ain't worth facing that one!"

"I wouldn't try it."

"It's unbelievable!"

The words rang in Bolt's brain. It's unbelievable, all right, he thought.

Five men dead. Six, counting Charley.

Senseless deaths. Necessary deaths.

Bolt walked back to his horse. He took fresh shells from his pocket, bent his head down to reload his pistol. When he looked up, Johnny Von was standing next to him.

"Thanks for the warning," Bolt said. "And thanks for taking out that third gunnie. I owe you one."

"Yeah. I didn't like the odds they were giving you. You all right?"

"I'm O.K."

Von acted like he was going to say something else. Instead, he turned and walked away.

Bolt mounted his horse and headed for home.

Riding down the main street, he saw all the glaring posters. A knot formed in the pit of his stomach as he realized the full impact of those posters. He knew he was the talk of the town now. He knew there would be those who would be afraid of him.

He also knew that there would be a few men left who thought they were fast enough to try for him again.

****

126

Major Horner heard the news from two of his men. He was standing outside in his yard, talking to his foreman, Luke Scarnes, when Nick Danvers and Jimmy Bill Yancy rode up.

Danvers and Yancy had been hitching their horses to the rail outside the Panhandle Club when they heard the first shot. They stood by their horses and watched the whole thing happen in front of the Brass Rail, which was right across the street. They had stayed around afterwards to find out all the details. They had learned that Bolt had already killed a man inside the Brass Rail a couple of hours earlier.

There was one thing that they didn't see, though. They hadn't seen Johnny Von crack off a shot from the porch. They thought Bolt had killed all the men himself.

"Bolt just killed six men in town," reported Nick Danvers.

"Yeah," said Jimmy Bill, "those posters sure brought 'em out of the bushes. There's a lot of 'em left who'd like to collect that bounty money."

Betsy was in her bedroom, upstairs, when she heard the commotion in the yard below. She walked over to the window, pulled the sheer curtain aside just enough to see who Major was talking to. The voices floated up to the open window. She let the curtain go, but stood silently by the window so she could hear the conversation.

"He's the fastest gun I ever saw," said Danvers.

"Yeah, he was nailing 'em three at a time," agreed Yancy.

"I don't see how any man could be that fast,"

said Horner.

"Well, he is," said Danvers. "His pistol's just a blur when he draws it. I swear those men were dead before he ever cleared leather."

"How'd it happen?" asked Horner.

Danvers explained every gory detail of how the gunmen were waiting for Bolt when he came out of the Brass Rail, how Bolt picked off the first two, then nailed the others when they rushed him.

"Well, he'll get careless one of these days. And when he does, when he lets his guard down, that's when he'll get his," said Horner.

"I sure wouldn't want to face Bolt's gun," said Jimmy Bill. "He's too durn fast. Don't think anyone else who witnessed it would want to face him either."

Horner didn't particularly like Jimmy Bill bragging about what a great gunman Bolt was. He cut him off sharp.

"I don't want any of my men in a shoot-out with Bolt right yet. Not that I don't think some of you could pick him off. I just don't want anyone connected with the Rocking H to be involved with his death. Let someone else kill him. You understand what I'm saying?"

"Yes, sir," said Jimmy Bill.

Danvers nodded.

"You go tell the other men here what I said."

Horner was infuriated by the turn of events. After Danvers and Yancy were gone, he took his rage out on Scarnes.

"Dammit, Luke. I don't like the way things are going. It looks like my plan is backfiring."

"Why?"

"Because if half the town saw Bolt in action, they'll be afraid to face his gun. Like Jimmy Bill said. I've got to have Bolt out of the picture. Whatever happened to that man you were supposed to hire to take care of Bolt?"

"He's coming. In his own time."

"Dammit, I want him here now. Who in hell is he?"

"You said you didn't want to know."

"All right, all right. But I'm out of patience. He should have been here a week ago if he's as good as you say he is."

"He's his own man. Does things in his own time. But, the important thing is he does them. When he agrees to get rid of a man, he gets rid of him. You don't have to worry about nothin'. It'll all be taken care of in time."

"I'm running out of time. I won't wait much longer for your man to show. If he ain't here in the next couple of days, we take matters into our own hands. Understand?"

"Yeah, yeah." Scarnes couldn't hide his irritation. He didn't like to be pushed around. He knew the man he had hired to do the job was the best there was. Dammit, why couldn't Horner have a little more patience? The hired gun would show up in a day or two.

"If your man isn't here by day after tomorrow, you better get Bolt yourself. After all, Bolt's a wanted man, an outlaw. He's fair game for any gun. We'd be doing the town a favor if we were to wipe him out. Yeah, set him up. Get him drunk. Get him in the bunk with some slut. Just get him!"

Horner turned and stomped away, disgusted that things weren't moving fast enough to suit him. He couldn't get that VeeBee property until Bolt was out of the way. Bolt had become a pebble in his boot. He wanted it removed.

Upstairs, Betsy turned away from the bedroom window. She had heard it all and she was scared. She walked over to her dressing table and sat down. She picked up her hair brush, stroked her long blonde hair idly.

Somehow she had to warn Bolt that her husband had given his ultimatum. Two more days and then Bolt would be killed for sure.

There was another reason she had to see Bolt. She had fallen in love with him all over again. It had been more than a week since Bolt had made love to her in the hotel room, and that's all she'd been able to think about since then. She felt like a real woman when she was with Bolt. She felt feminine and sensuous when she was close to him. Loved and loving. He did that to her. Brought out the best in her.

She hadn't wanted Horner to touch her since she'd been with Bolt. When Horner had made his demands on her she was not able to perform her obligatory wifely duties. She claimed a headache or illness and asked his forgiveness. Let him get his sex from the prostitutes, the women he kept on the side.

She didn't know how long she could go on like this. Loving one man for his gentleness, hating her own husband for his crudeness. She wished she could run away from it all. She dreamed of leaving her husband and going to some place far away with Bolt. It wouldn't work, she knew, at least not now.

She would go see Bolt tomorrow afternoon, beg him again to leave town. Maybe she could join him some day.

Tears welled up in her eyes when she thought about Bolt. She couldn't bear it if he were to die. And yet, she knew his time was almost up if he didn't leave right away. He couldn't go around hiding from people, or killing everyone who decided to go after him for the reward money. That was no way to live and sometime, somewhere, as Major had said, someone would catch him off guard. And then he would be gone forever.

****

It was mid-afternoon the following day when Luke Scarnes spotted Elizabeth out by the stable. She was standing next to her saddled horse. He watched her pull her long hair back and put a wide-brimmed hat on.

She untied her horse from the post, put a foot in the stirrup, pulled herself up. She wore brown riding pants, a matching jacket. The yellow bow on her blouse was neatly tied at her neck.

She looked like a woman with class, Scarnes thought. He'd known a woman like that once, a classy lady. He'd loved her very deeply. And she'd loved him, too, until that day he'd gotten pistol-whipped. After that she couldn't stand to look at his scarred face.

Maybe that's why he hated Elizabeth so much. She reminded him of the only woman he had ever loved.

Luke had watched Elizabeth with eagle eyes for

more than a week. This was the first time she left the house since Moss the Mouth had told him about her scandalous affair. He knew she was going to meet her lover. He just didn't know who it was. He'd find out soon enough. Then he could tell Major what his pretty little wife was up to behind his back.

Scarnes stood in the shadow of the barn, watched as Elizabeth rode away from the stable. He waited until she was out of sight before he went for his own horse. He figured she was headed for town, to rendezvous with her lover at the same hotel Moss had told him about.

He held back when he got to the road, keeping a safe distance between them.

When Betsy reached the fork in the road, she took the south fork.

"Where the hell is she going?" he thought. "Town's the other way."

Once she got some distance away from the ranch, she left the main road. She cut across the open field, disappeared into the trees that lined the river. For a few moments, Luke thought she might just be out riding for the fresh air or to get away from the house for the afternoon. She was on VeeBee property now.

He rode up to a tall tree, brought his horse to a halt. He kept in the shadows, watched Elizabeth cross the river. The river was shallow there. The water covered only about five or six inches of her horse's legs.

When she had crossed the river, she kicked her horse in the flanks, sped up the hill.

Once, when she was out in the open, she stopped her horse and looked behind her. It was almost as if she knew someone was following her.

Luke stayed in the shadows of the trees. He knew she couldn't see him.

Elizabeth took off in a hurry. She headed directly toward the VeeBee Ranch.

Luke wondered who she was going to see.

He had to know.

CHAPTER THIRTEEN

"Bolt, it just isn't worth it," said Belle.

"It's the principal of the thing at this point," he argued.

"No. I don't want to be responsible for your death. I wish I'd never asked you to help me. I'd rather lose this damn ranch than see you dead. I didn't think anybody would be hunting you way out here in Oklahoma. But now look what's happened. Those damn posters plastered all over town. Your life is in danger. All those men you had to kill yesterday afternoon. That's all people talked about at work last night. About what a fast gun you are."

"Maybe that'll give some of them second thoughts about coming after me."

Belle was ready to go back to town for another night's work at the Panhandle Club. Ginny was inside waiting for her. They hadn't known about the killings until they got to work the night before. Belle became extremely upset when she heard the customers talking about the afternoon blood bath.

"No, I heard them talking," she said. "Someone else will try it, even if they have to get drunk to get up enough courage."

"You let me worry about that, Belle."

"I give up," she sighed. "You're the stubbornest man I've ever known. I've got to get going. Ginny's waiting for me. We're going to do some shopping this afternoon. I dread going to work tonight. I hate that damned job."

"That's what it's all about, isn't it, Belle? You and Ginny should be free to work this ranch like you want to without having to work half the night performing for those drunken slobs. Horner's made it impossible for you to do that. He hasn't been bothering you since I came around, has he?"

"No, but . . ."

"No buts. I'm here because you needed help and I aim to stay until this thing's settled."

"Be careful, will you, Bolt?" She turned away so he wouldn't see the tears that were welling up in her eyes.

"I will."

"See you later."

A few minutes later, Bolt waved at the two girls as they rode off. Tom had gone to town a little earlier to get some needed supplies. He wouldn't be home for a couple of hours.

Bolt was alone at the ranch.

****

She cursed under her breath when she rode up on her black stallion. Kathleen Gallihan saw her father and Dennis out by the stable. Right where she had to go. She had hoped to ride up quietly, sneak into her

135

bedroom without anyone seeing her. Her face was bruised and she didn't want to face anyone right now. She hated the thought of having to explain the bruises.

She rode on in, keeping the hat that covered her long red hair tilted at an angle so that it shaded most of her face.

Paddy looked up as she stopped her black horse a few feet away.

"Afternoon, sweetheart. Where've you been?"

"Good afternoon, Father. I've just been out riding in the country."

And then he saw her face. The cut and puffy lip, the laceration on her cheek.

"Kathleen, your face! What happened?" He walked over to her, took a closer look. His stomach turned when he saw the extent of her bruises.

"I got thrown from my horse," she lied. "Hit my face on a rock."

"Blackie threw you? He's as gentle as they come."

"He got spooked by a rattlesnake. I fell off when he bucked." She avoided eye contact with her cousin, Dennis.

"Oh, honey," said Paddy, "that's terrible." Her father wrapped his arm around her. "We'll get you inside and take care of you."

"I'm all right, Father. Just a little sore. I want to take care of Blackie. Get him unsaddled and fed."

"I'll help her, Paddy," said Dennis. "You go on inside."

Dennis waited until they were alone.

"Kind of early for rattlers, isn't it?" said Dennis.

"Well . . . maybe it wasn't a . . ."

136

"What really happened, Kate?"

"Just what I said. Blackie got spooked."

"I don't buy it, Kate. Horner did that to you, didn't he?"

Kathleen's eyes shot up at Dennis. Her mouth fell open in shock.

"How . . . wha . . ." she stammered.

"Don't lie to me, Kate. I know all about you and Horner."

"How could you?" She brought her hand up to her face, twisted her long red hair nervously.

"I suspected something was going on a couple of weeks ago. You started acting strange, kind of distant. We've been close for a long time and suddenly you seem like you're trying to avoid me. I was in town one day and saw you going into the Cimarron Hotel."

"Lots of people go in there. Sometimes I have lunch there with a friend."

"Look, Kate, I know you met Horner there. I just don't understand why."

Kathleen lowered her head and began to sob.

"Oh, it's been so terrible. He made me do it. I didn't want to."

"How could he force you?"

"He . . . he saw us . . . that day we were out by the river. He saw us . . . he saw everything."

"That's none of his business."

"He told me it was wrong. What we were doing. He said it was incest. He threatened to tell my folks about us if I didn't meet him."

"It isn't incest, and you know it. Not really. I was adopted when I was a baby. You know that and your

137

folks know it. We're not related by blood lines, only by coincidence. What difference does it make if your parents know how we feel about each other?"

"I guess it doesn't. I just thought they wouldn't understand."

"How long have you and Horner . . . been seeing each other?"

"I've only been with him twice before today. I hate that man. He's so cruel."

"Why did he beat you today?"

"He wanted me to tell him what Bolt was up to. I told him I didn't know anything about what Bolt was doing or planned to do. I told him I hardly knew Bolt. That's the truth. I've only met him once. Horner didn't believe me. He said his men had seen you and Mike and Father working over at the VeeBee."

"That's not something you go beating up a woman for."

"That's not why he hit me. He wanted to use me to help set Bolt up. He said he wanted me to come on strong with Bolt, get him in bed so they could trap him and kill him. I told Horner I wouldn't have anything to do with such a plan. That's when he slapped me. He told me I was a . . . well, he called me names. He said he'd tell my folks all about me if I refused to cooperate. I'm so scared of him."

"That dirty bastard. I'd like to kill him with my bare hands."

"Don't talk that way. He'd have you killed in a minute if he knew I told you that he beat me. He said he'd kill me if I told anyone. He's crazy, Dennis." She wiped away the tears that streamed down her cheeks.

"You're safe now, Kate. You won't ever have to see him again. I love you very much, you know. I think it's time we tell your parents how we feel about each other. I'm sure they'll understand."

"Don't tell them about Horner and me. Please."

"I won't. This will always be our secret."

She lowered her head.

"I don't see how you can still love me knowing that I . . . that Horner . . ."

"Don't think about it anymore, Kate. It happened and it's over with. I'll always love you."

****

Bolt looked up when he heard the pounding hoofbeats coming his way.

He didn't recognize the rider or the horse, but someone was hellbent for leather. One thing for sure. No gunnie in his right mind would ride in so bold.

It wasn't until Elizabeth was a hundred yards away that Bolt realized that the rider was a woman. He saw the long blonde hair blowing in the breeze, knew it was Betsy.

She rode up fast and climbed down from her horse.

"What brings you to enemy territory?" he asked.

"Bolt, they're planning to kill you!" Her words came in gasps. She was out of breath from pushing her horse so fast.

"What else is new?"

"I'm serious. Major has given orders to have you killed."

"He gave that order a long time ago."

139

"You don't realize how serious it is. You've got to get away from here. Please!"

"I will. In my own time. In my own way."

"He's going to trick you. He won't rest until you're dead."

"I'm not worried."

"You're impossible, Bolt!" Betsy stuck her hands on her hips, tossed her hair back with the flip of her head.

"You got a stubborn streak in you, don't you?" grinned Bolt.

"You're the stubborn one. You're a jackass."

"I been called worse."

"How can you just stand there and stay so calm? Don't you have any feelings?"

"I reckon I got as many fears as the next man. It just doesn't do any good to worry. A man could worry his life away. Fear has crippled many a good man. I take life as it comes. Good or bad."

"I can see I'm not going to be able to pound any sense into that thick head of yours."

"Nope."

There was nothing else to say.

She stood there, shaking her head, wanting to take her frustrations out on something. In a way, she felt betrayed. She had risked a lot to sneak away from her house and ride over here to warn Bolt. He wouldn't even listen to her.

Suddenly, she threw her arms around him, held him tight. Her body trembled against his.

"Don't worry about me, Betsy."

"I love you, Bolt. I can't help but worry." She stepped back away from him. "I shouldn't even be here, I know. I hope the girls don't see me. I doubt they'd appreciate having a Horner on their land."

"Who? Belle and Ginny? They've already gone to town. Won't be back till morning. Nobody's here but me."

She looked up at him with pleading blue eyes.

"Bolt, I want you. Could we . . . ?"

Betsy's boldness surprised Bolt. It would be different if they were someplace other than here. Out in the woods, like the first time, or in a hotel.

"Let's go on in the house," he said.

She felt uncomfortable once they were inside the rambling ranch house. It wasn't nearly as elegant as her own home, but she liked it. There was a homey atmosphere to it that hers lacked. She could feel the presence of the two women who lived there, women she knew only by sight.

There was a sweet clean smell to the house. Lavender instead of stale cigars.

"You sleep in here?" she asked, jealousy tugging at her heart.

"Sometimes. Sometimes in the bunkhouse."

He led her down a long hallway to one of two bedrooms that was at the back of the house. The other bedrooms were at the front of the house, one on either side of the livingroom. The house was originally a two room cabin with rooms tacked on in a hit-or-miss fashion as they were needed.

Betsy's eyes darted around the room as if she was looking for something. She saw some of Bolt's clothing hanging in a curtained closet, saw other of his belongings scattered about the room.

"I'm surprised you sleep in the house," she said.

141

"Usually the hired hands stay in a bunkhouse." She tried to act casual about it. She took her hat off, set it on the dresser.

"Yeah, they usually do," he smiled.

She started to undress, fumbled nervously with a button on her riding jacket. She took it off, folded it neatly and hung it over the back of a straight chair. Her curiosity finally got the best of her.

"Damn it, Bolt. What's between you and Miss Hammond? Or is it Miss Darling? Or both?"

"We're old friends. Belle and me. It's a long story."

She knew he wasn't going to tell her any more. It really didn't matter. She was with him now and that was all she cared about.

She untied the bow of her blouse, undid the buttons. She undressed, draped her clothes over her jacket. She moved close to Bolt.

"Nice," he said, cupping a breast in his hand as if to weigh it as he would a melon. He kissed her tenderly, probing her mouth with his tongue. She responded by thrusting her thighs into his, rubbing them against him in a gyrating motion. He slid his hand down her bare back, pulled on her smooth buttocks, shoving her crotch up tight against him.

She gasped when she felt the bulge in his pants press against her.

"I want you so much." Her voice was low, husky.

"Climb in bed."

He undressed quickly, moved to the bed.

"You're ready so soon," she said, admiring his swollen wavering erection.

"Are you?"

"Yes, I'm ready."

He pushed her gently over on the bed, crawled in beside her. He ran his hand across her soft flesh, stopping at her breasts to caress them. She gasped when his hand reached her inner thighs, lingered there. He traced a path around her furry mound, slid his finger across the sex portal. He felt the dampness, the warmth.

She took his rigid shaft in her hand, squeezed it.

"I want you inside me," she whispered. "Deep inside."

Her words caused an involuntary twitch in his cock.

She felt a need to hurry, although she would rather spend a long time playing with Bolt, having him play with her. She couldn't shake the thought that she was in another woman's home. She felt like they were being watched.

Once Bolt slid into her honey pot, she forgot about time and place. She became a wild tiger, not caring where she was. She was every bit a woman as she bounced and bucked, thrashed beneath Bolt. She spread her legs wide, threw them up in the air, wrapped them around his buttocks.

Bolt sank in deeper with the new position. He rammed her to the hilt, felt her gripping muscles tug at his stalk. She was like a small girl desperate for affection. She was a grown woman, sure of her sexuality. She was a wanton hussy, flaunting her wares. She was one woman. She was all women.

Bolt's excitement mounted as he plumbed her deep. Her muscles tightened around his organ with every stroke, locking him inside the steaming cauldron. It was as if she was sucking him down into a deep, wet, swirling darkness that was all sweetness and softness, velvet and silk. A whirlpool of pleasure and heat, of total power.

He couldn't last. He was pulled into the pool as he exploded with a mindless orgasm. He shuddered against her as his milky seed spewed from his gushing fountain. He grunted and groaned. Animal sounds. He held her tight until the throbbing slowed down and ceased. The thrashing stopped, the bucking and twisting. The slapping of skin against skin stopped. The room became silent. Only the sound of racing, pounding hearts remained. It was a time of complete satisfaction. For both of them.

Betsy's words broke the silence.

"I've got to get out of here in a hurry," she said, sliding out of bed.

"What's your hurry? The girls won't be back until morning."

"It's not that. I shouldn't even be here. I can't be away from home too long." She reached for her clothes, dressed quickly.

"I wish you could stay."

"Me too, but I can't." She grabbed her hat from the dresser, looked in the mirror as she plunked it on her head.

"Just a minute. I'll walk out with you."

Bolt slipped into his clothes, didn't bother to smooth out his hair.

He heard the noise when he stepped outside.

Hoofbeats.

Going away from the house, just over the rise.

Someone had been there.

Someone who didn't want to be seen!

144

CHAPTER FOURTEEN

Bolt held up a hand, cocked his head to listen.

"Hear that?" he asked.

"Just barely," said Betsy. "Sounds like a horse in the distance."

"Yeah. Riding away from here."

Betsy's eyebrows shot up. "What's that supposed to mean?"

"Did anyone follow you here, Betsy?"

"I don't think so. I checked my backtrail once. I didn't see anybody."

Bolt took a couple of steps, his head lowered. He walked a bit farther, his eyes scanning the ground. He stepped carefully until he found what he was looking for.

Hoofprints. Where no horse should have been. He followed them, saw where the rider had sat his horse for a short time. The tracks led Bolt around the house to the back. They ended near the bedroom window. Bolt's bedroom window.

He saw the boot marks then. The slight impressions in the dry dirt where the rider had dismounted to get closer to the window. He saw the broken and crushed branches of a bush under the window. Someone had moved in close to the house.

Bolt's eyes shot to the window. The curtains were drawn. Nobody could have seen into the bedroom. But the window was open. Whoever had been standing there had gotten his ears full.

Bolt thought for a moment that it could have been someone out to pick up some quick bounty money, but dismissed the thought. If someone had been after the reward money, he could have stuck around and shot him when he came outside. No. Not a bounty hunter.

"Betsy, someone followed you here."

"I didn't see anyone."

"He didn't want you to see him. I'm going to ride back with you."

"Bolt, you can't ride over there to my place!" She was horrified by the idea.

"I'll ride a ways. I want to check it out."

They mounted their horses and rode slowly. Bolt checked the tracks as they went, followed them through the brush, the open grazing land. The tracks led to the river.

"This the way you rode when you came over?"

"Yes," she said, "but I crossed the river down there by that tree. I remember that tree because it's crooked." She pointed to a place twenty-five feet from where they were.

Bolt climbed down off Nick, studied the sign.

"Well, someone else crossed right here, and not very long ago. Look at those stones in the water. Most of them are covered by green slime. But look at

146

those." He stooped down and pointed to the rocks that shimmered in the sunlight. "The horse's hooves scraped the slime off of those, turned some over. Someone's getting mighty nosey."

"I'd better get home right away, Bolt. You go on back. I'll be all right."

"Ride careful. If anything happens, scream as loud as you can. I'll wait here until I think you're home."

She let her horse pick his way across the shallow river. Once she got to the other side, she turned and waved at Bolt. She spurred her horse in the flanks and took off at a gallop.

****

Horner called to her when she entered the house.

"Elizabeth? Is that you?"

"Yes, Major," she called back from the hallway.

"Come here a minute."

She walked down the hall to his study, stood in the doorway.

"Where have you been?" he asked.

"Out riding. It was such a beautiful day and I wanted some fresh air." She avoided looking him in the eye.

"Hope you enjoyed your outing."

"Yes, I did." She tried to calm the butterflies in her stomach. She felt bare, naked, as if he could see right through her.

"Here. This came for you today." He held a letter out to her.

She recognized the handwriting immediately.

147

It was her father's.

"Thank you." She turned and started to walk away.

"Aren't you going to open it?"

"Yes, of course. It's from my father."

"Oh."

Betsy's eyes darted up to Major's. He had been suspicious because she had received a letter and he didn't know who it was from.

It wasn't like her father to write letters. She opened it slowly, fearing that it contained bad news.

Major turned away, slightly embarrassed by his suspicions.

She read the letter quickly to herself. It was short, to the point.

"Father's coming for a visit. Listen." She read the letter again. This time aloud.

"Dear Elizabeth, I am passing through Black Mesa on Friday, the 18th. Would like to see you and meet your husband, Major. Meet me in town at noon. I'll buy you both lunch. Your loving father."

"That's good. I've wanted to meet him. Glad he's coming." Major gave his wife an affectionate hug. He towered over her.

"Friday! That's tomorrow!" She was so excited about her father's visit that she forgot all about the man who had followed her to the VeeBee Ranch.

****

It was late afternoon when Betsy went out to feed her horse. It was something she wouldn't let anyone else do. That was her only real possession. She had

148

jewels and trinkets that her husband had given her. She had beautiful hand-sewn dresses and polished furniture. Everything she wanted or needed. But they were cold things that went with her position in life. It was her horse that was real and warm and responded to her attention.

She always fed him at this time. Shortly before she sat down to supper with Major.

She had changed out of her riding clothes. She wore a long blue gown that accented the color of her eyes. Her blonde hair was neatly brushed.

She jumped a foot when Luke Scarnes spoke to her. She hadn't seen him standing in the shadow of the stable when she walked up. He stepped away from the building.

"Hello, Elizabeth." His words were drawn out, accentuated.

"Oh! You startled me . . ." She didn't care much for Luke. Never had. There was something unwholesome about him. She had gotten used to his scarred face. That didn't bother her any more. It was his manner, the greasy look about him, his sneakiness. She avoided him whenever possible. She knew the feeling was mutual. They hadn't liked each other since the first time they had met, which was two days after she had married Major. Luke had worked for Major for five years before she came into the picture. She figured Luke wouldn't have liked any girl Horner had chosen for a wife. Luke wanted to be the big shot in Major's life. A wife only complicated things.

"What have you got to be scared about?" he asked.

"Nothing. I just didn't see you."

"I think you got plenty to be scared about, Elizabeth. Or should I call you Betsy?"

She froze when she heard the word Betsy. Only Bolt called her that. Luke. Of course. He would be the one to follow her. Her face turned red with anger.

"You . . . you . . ." she stuttered.

"Yes, me. I know all about you and your boyfriend."

"You don't know anything," she snapped.

"I heard everything that went on with you two love birds this afternoon. I found it quite interesting. I also know about the afternoon you visited him at the hotel room. You should be more careful, Betsy."

"You're the scum of the earth," she spat.

"Now, that's no way to talk to a nice, law abiding feller like me."

"Leave me alone!"

"I think Major will be interested to find out his little wifie has a boyfriend. Especially when he finds out who the boyfriend is. Major might get real riled up when he finds out he's not man enough to take care of his little woman and that she has to find someone else to pleasure her."

"You dirty . . ."

"Oh, no, I don't think Major will be very happy at all when I tell him you got yourself an outlaw lover."

She turned her head away, brought her hands up to her mouth. A sickening knot formed in the pit of her stomach.

"'Course it might make him hate Bolt a little more. Major might just go right out and kill Bolt himself when I tell him what you two been doing."

He paused, let his words sink in.

"Maybe I won't tell your husband. At least not yet. Depends on you, little lady."

She whirled on him, brought tiny fists up shoulder high. She wanted to scratch his eyes out, kick him in the groin. Her body trembled with anger, with hatred for the treacherous man who was her husband's closest friend. She brought her hands down to her waist, pushed against her stomach. She tried to control the shaking, the nausea that boiled in her stomach.

Luke's mouth curled to a cruel smile. He was getting the reaction from Elizabeth he wanted.

"What do you want from me?" she snapped.

"Not much. I want you to leave Major. For good. Go back to teaching little ones their reading and writing. Major don't need you. You're an anchor around his neck. You drag him down."

Her face blanched ashen. Her knees became rubbery appendages.

"Leave town right away," he continued, "and I don't say anything to Major."

"That's blackmail!" she glared.

"Call it what you want. If you don't move out, I spill the beans about you and Bolt. Don't know what Major will do when he finds out about your cheating ways with that outlaw." He raised his hat off his head, slid it back on. "I'd sure hate to kindle Major's wrath if I were you. He's got a mighty mean temper. He just might want to kill you along with your boyfriend. Think about it."

She fought to keep down the bile that rose to her throat. In an effort to control her trembling, her fingernails dug into the skin of her other hand.

151

It wouldn't make any difference anyway, she knew. Her father was coming to town tomorrow and he would be sure to tell Major about Bolt. And her. Her father was that way. He always interfered in her life. She thought it might be different now that she was married. But she wasn't so sure. She loved her father very much, wanted him to meet her husband, but she was also frightened by it.

She cringed when she thought about her predicament. Her world was collapsing around her and there was nothing she could do about it.

She knew Luke was right about her husband. Major would probably kill her if he found out about her and Bolt. And he would surely kill Bolt. Luke had her over a barrel.

One thing, she knew, she wouldn't give Luke Scarnes the satisfaction of giving into his demands. She'd take her chances, live with the consequences.

"Tell Major what you wish," she snorted. "He won't believe you anyway." She turned away from him, went inside the corral, picked up a bucket and dipped into the feed bin.

"You'll be sorry, little lady. You better think again about what I said." He walked toward the house, secure with his secret that he would use if he had to. He was sure he wouldn't have to tell Horner. She'd think it over, come to her senses.

Betsy shuddered after he was gone. She'd called his bluff. The next move was his.

* * * * * * * *

Bolt walked through the town like he owned it.

His steps were brisk, his eyes alert. His hand hung loosely at his side, ready to reach for his pistol in a flash, if he needed to.

He felt the eyes on him as he walked from the livery stable, where he'd left his horse to have its shoes trimmed, to the Cherokee Hotel.

It was almost ten in the morning.

He would be on time for his appointment with Belle and Ginny.

Tom got to the ranch the day before shortly after Bolt returned from escorting Betsy to the river. Bolt had waited at the river for about twenty minutes before he returned to the ranch. He figured Betsy had made it home without any trouble. At least she hadn't screamed for help.

Tom had given Bolt a message from Belle and Ginny. Something about Belle wanting to sell out, give up the ranch. Tom said she sounded pretty hysterical. Belle asked Tom to tell Bolt to come in and meet them in the dining room at the Cherokee at ten this morning.

Bolt knew it was important or she wouldn't have asked.

He kept his head straight ahead as he walked the block and a half to the Cherokee, but his eyes darted from place to place, watching for any sudden movement that might spell trouble. He felt the eyes on him as he passed the falsefronts in town. He heard the whispers, the mutterings from small clusters of men in the street. He saw the wanted posters, still tacked to everything that didn't move, some of them beginning to fade from exposure to the bright sun.

Nobody called him out.

Nobody shot him in the back.

For once, he was glad his reputation went before him.

He stepped inside the Cherokee Hotel, stopped in the lobby long enough to take a deep breath. It seemed he had held his breath for the past ten minutes, the time it took him to get from the livery stable to the hotel.

The dining room was practically empty at that time of day. There were a few stragglers eating a late breakfast, a few others enjoying mid-morning coffee. Bolt glanced around the room, saw Ginny sitting at a window table. She wasn't hard to spot with her long dark hair. She was the tallest woman in the room.

He walked over and sat down across the table from her.

"Morning, Ginny. Where's Belle?"

"She's not feeling well. She asked me to talk to you."

"Anything serious?"

"No, I don't think so. She's just worn herself to a frazzle worrying over that ranch. She's talking about selling out again. She wants to quit, give up."

"You, too?"

"Hell no. I'll fight to the end if it's worth fighting for. We've worked too hard to get where we are to give up now."

"I like your spunk, Ginny," he smiled.

It was a compliment and she didn't know how to accept it. She was usually full of wise cracks, a mechanism she used to keep people, especially men, from getting through the wall she had built around herself. Right now, she was at a loss for words.

"Would you like to go up to my room for a drink?" he asked.

"Only a drink?" There was sarcasm in her voice. She knew what he meant by the invitation.

"Depends on you, Ginny."

"Pushy, aren't you?"

"I don't push. Not with a lady. I ask, sometimes."

"Are you asking?"

"One way to put it. I reckon I asked you the first time I saw you."

CHAPTER FIFTEEN

It would have been closer to go to Ginny's room. It was just upstairs. But Belle was in the room next to Ginny's, trying to sleep, trying to regain control of her emotions.

Ginny couldn't explain why she felt the way she did about Bolt. She had felt the attraction the first time she met him. The magnetism, the charm. It wasn't that he was handsome, because he wasn't particularly. He was rugged. He was his own man.

She had fought against her feelings for a long time. She didn't even know how to accept a relationship with a man anymore. After she left her husband, who was extremely cruel to her, she kept a healthy distance between herself and other men. She now realized that she had been punishing herself, for no good reason.

She was ready for a man's love.

She was ready for Bolt.

****

Moss the Mouth had been paid in advance. For

what he did best: spying.

It was easy. All he had to do was watch and see if Bolt came to town. There'd be a bonus in it if Bolt showed. He'd collect that when he reported to the man who was paying him. Nick Danvers.

From his spot in front of the Dunfee's General Store, Moss could see everyone who came or went. He'd spent so much time sweeping the boardwalk in front of the store, the wooden planks were wearing thin.

Bolt showed. Finally. Moss watched him ride into town, stop at the livery stable, then walk directly to the Cherokee Hotel. A few minutes later, Moss saw Bolt emerge from the hotel with Miss Darling.

The town snoop kept his head lowered, swept the boardwalk with a renewed vigor as Bolt and his lady friend passed by him. He looked up again, leaned on the broom, watched the couple cross the street. A few doors down, Bolt turned into the Cimarron Hotel.

Moss knew that Bolt would be there a while. A man didn't take a pretty gal like Ginny to the Cimarron unless he planned to spend some time with her.

It was time to report to Danvers, collect his bonus.

****

Bolt's room was on the ground floor, at the rear of the hotel. It was sparsely furnished as most hotel rooms were. Bolt kept only one change of clothes in the room. A small satchel in the corner held a few emergency items. Beef jerky, a bottle of whiskey, extra tobacco, sulphur matches. The rest of his things were out at the ranch.

157

"You want whiskey?" he asked. "It's all I got."

"Not really, thanks. It's too early." When she smiled, small indentations dimpled her cheeks.

"Well, I'll be damned. You got dimples. I love dimples!"

She laughed, then moved close to him, brushed his lips with her own. She was tall, only a few inches shorter than Bolt.

"It's the truth. Odd I never noticed them before. Don't think I've ever seen you smile."

"I'll have to change that."

"I heard tell that women with dimples were good . . . ah, partners."

"You mean in bed?"

"Could be."

"You want to find out?"

Bolt melted under her hot sultry stare.

She came to him like some starved animal, clinging, begging for affection. She wrapped her arms around him, nuzzled her nose in his neck.

He drew her tight, held her for a long moment. He put his fingers under her chin, lifted her head. Kissed her tenderly on the mouth. Her lips were warm, moist. She pressed her tall, slender body against him.

"You're beautiful, Ginny," he husked.

He brought his hands up, started unbuttoning her dress. The buttons went all the way to the hem. He didn't bother with all of them, just enough so that he could slip the gown off her shoulders. He ran his hands across the bare flesh of her shoulders, put them around behind her and fiddled with the fastener of her brassiere.

"Never was very good with these."

She let him struggle with it. When he finally got the clasp undone, she pulled the straps down over her arms, slipped them off and dropped the bra on the floor. Her large breasts, free of the cloth confinement, jutted out, bare, bold, tantalizing.

Bolt took one of them in his hand, bent his head to kiss her there. The nipple hardened in his mouth.

She took a step backwards, let her dress fall to the floor in a heap, then stepped out of it. She stood before him wearing only sheer white panties which accentuated her long graceful legs. She would wait, let Bolt take them off.

He felt the tug at his manhood as it began to swell against the tight restraint of his Levi's. He took his gun belt off, hung his holster on the bedpost. It was only a minute before he was naked, his erection full blown.

She eyed his rigid organ with awe.

"Come on," she said, "I want to do things to you." She took his hand, led him to the bed.

"You're fast—when you get going."

"I know a good thing when I see it."

Bolt reached over and threw the covers back. She pulled him onto the bed. She didn't let go of him until he was right beside her.

"You need these?" he said, reaching for her panties.

"Not now."

He propped himself up on one elbow, leaned over to kiss her. His tongue slid in past her moist lips, explored her warm mouth.

She put her hand to his crotch, found his manhood. She took it in her hand, massaged it. Her fingers tightened around it, moved up and down its length.

Bolt's hand traced a path down her long body, stopping at her full breasts to fondle them before he searched for her sex cleft. He ran his hands across her flat tummy, between her thighs. He rubbed her thighs, was fascinated by her long legs. His finger slid across her slit. He felt the dampness.

"You want me, Ginny?" His voice was low, scratchy.

"Yes, but not yet. I want to enjoy you first. Every inch of you." She pushed on his shoulders, tipped him back so that he was flat on his back. "Do you mind?"

"Be my guest."

She started at the shoulders, massaging them with a firm grip. Her hands moved to his upper arms where she squeezed the flesh to relax his muscles. When she ran her fingertips lightly over his hairy chest, across his bare tummy, it sent tiny shivers through him. Goose bumps stippled his bare skin.

Her hand touched his swollen member. It twitched in her hand. She stroked it, moving her fingers up and down its throbbing length.

He thrust his hips up, moaned.

"That feel good?"

"Unh huh."

"That's only the beginning," she teased.

She twisted her body around, brought her head down to his loins. She lapped at the sticky fluid that leaked from the tiny slit, tasted the lemony flavor. She held the base of his cock in her hand, brought her mouth around the bell-shaped head. Her lips opened wider as she took the whole length of his organ into her mouth.

She bobbed up and down, pressing her lips against his tight, veined skin. She sucked until her cheeks hollowed. She went slow. She went fast. Her touch was expert, exquisite.

She slipped her free hand under his buttocks, clamped it tight on one cheek. Her head rocked back and forth as she swallowed him with a hungry suckling. She pulled on him until her jaws ached. She drew his organ out of her mouth so her lips covered only his mushroomed head. With her tongue, she traced a circle around the flared tip. Her tongue became a hard probe as she tried to stick it in the tiny slit.

Bolt's seed began to boil. He struggled to keep from exploding in her mouth.

She knew he was getting close to orgasm. It was too soon. She backed off, drawing his cock out of her mouth.

She scooted over on top of him, straddled his legs. She lowered herself on his skewer. The head of his cock was wet with her saliva. It slid in easily. She pushed down until he filled her completely.

"Ohh, ohhhh, ohhhh," she cried as the first orgasm shook her.

A moment later, she was thrashing and bucking on him like a wanton. She released emotions she had kept bottled up for years. She was a free woman again.

She continued her thrashing as the orgasms came, one after another.

Bolt held back, letting her have her head, allowing her to satisfy her needs. Finally, when she slowed down, he rolled her over on her back."

"Let me get between your legs," he said.

"Yes, oh yes."

He looked down at her dark thatch, bent to kiss it. Her musk added to his excitement. He rolled his tongue around the folds of her portal. He jabbed his tongue inside, deep as he could. He felt her hips rise to meet him.

He moved up and over her body, his shaft aimed at her sex cleft. She spread her legs wider to accept him. He sunk into her warm sheath, felt her muscles tighten around him.

He stroked her slow, deep, basking in the warmth of her velvet cove. She thrust her eager loins up to meet him every time he plunged in deep. Her rhythm matched his exactly, no matter whcther he stroked her fast or slow. He felt in complete harmony with her.

He kissed her open mouth, delighting in her passionate response to his love making. He felt her firm breasts crush against his bare chest. He closed his eyes and thought of her long slender legs. She was some woman, this one. She was all woman. She had a strange power over him. Normally, he wouldn't have lasted this long, but she was able to keep him going by moving with him to such a degree that he felt they were one. He had the feeling he could go on for hours at this pace; at this delicate point of sheer ecstasy that comes to a man just before he spills his seed.

She had the power and yet she made him feel powerful.

The time was right. They moved together as he stroked her deeply. He built up slowly, a little more with each deep thrust. He felt her body tremble with orgasm.

"Now," he said. "Now."

He pushed hard into the bottom of her lush pit. He held her tight as his seed erupted inside her.

He lingered awhile before he rolled off her. He lay next to her, folded his hands behind his head so that his arms formed small wings.

Neither of them said anything for a long time.

Bolt thought about Ginny. It would be easy to fall in love with her. She was the kind he'd pick if he was a settling man. But he wasn't.

Finally, he turned to her and smiled.

"You're the best, Ginny."

"You do that to me, Bolt. Bring out the best." Her cheeks dimpled when she smiled. She got out of bed, started to dress. "You know what I wish?"

"What's that?"

"I wish we could spend a whole night together sometime. So we could enjoy each other without being hurried. So that we could fall asleep, snuggle to each other all night."

"I owe you one, Ginny. That's a promise."

"I'll be right back. I want to freshen up a little. Where is the bathroom?"

"It's at the end of the hall, on the right."

Her blood froze in her veins when she stepped out in the hall. There were two men there, one to her left, the other across the hall, two doors down. She recognized both of them. Nick Danvers and Jimmy Bill Yancy. Horner's men. Both of them had harrassed her and Belle at the Panhandle Club.

The men turned away when they saw her, tried to act casual. Danvers turned the handle on the door where he was standing, pretended he was going inside. Yancy walked on down the hall. She didn't miss the pistols they had drawn.

She ducked back into the room, her face ashen.

Bolt was stepped into his trousers when she came back in. He looked at her, saw the fear in her eyes.

"There are two men out there," she whispered, "in the hall. Horner's men. They're waiting for you, Bolt. They've got pistols drawn."

"Sonofabitch," he muttered.

He thought quickly.

"You stay here, Ginny. Stay low. Behind the bed."

He grabbed his pistol from its holster, checked it. He dashed to the window, opened it quietly. It stuck half way up. He couldn't squeeze through the small opening.

"Damn it!"

"What are you going to do?" Her voice was shaky.

"Never mind. Just do what I told you to." He cursed the fact he hadn't left a spare rifle in the closet so she could protect herself if she needed to.

She ran to the far side of the bed, away from the door. She crouched down, watched Bolt struggle with the window.

He tried to force the window open. It wouldn't budge. He lowered it slightly, then began tapping upward on each side with the palm of his hand. He eased it up a little at a time. Finally, he got it past the point where it was sticking. It shot up.

He stuck one leg through the window, ducked his head low.

"Be careful, Bolt," Ginny whispered.

He pulled himself through the window, dropped to the ground.

And then he was gone.

All Ginny could do was pray.

CHAPTER SIXTEEN

There was no one in the alley behind the hotel.

Bolt was shirtless, barefooted.

He had to go through the lobby. There was no other way.

He dashed around the building, to the front. He checked to both sides of him before he stepped inside. Just in case.

He walked quickly through the lobby, his gun held flat against his leg, pointing down at the floor. He ignored the stares of the desk clerk. Joe Carter started to say something, changed his mind.

Bolt headed straight for the back hall.

He slowed down when he neared the corner where the hall made a right angle turn. His bare feet made no sound at all.

He snugged himself against the wall, peeked around the corner.

They were still there. Waiting for him outside his room.

Danvers was crouched low, on one side of the door, his back to Bolt. His pistol was aimed at the doorknob.

An easy shot. But Bolt didn't back shoot a man.

Yancy stood on the other side of the door, his back flattened against the wall.

There was no way a man could come out through that door and walk away alive.

Bolt stepped out into the hallway. On silent feet.

"You lookin' for me?" he called.

Danvers whirled around, shot from a crouched position.

Bolt ducked, sidestepped the bullet. It whizzed by his arm, spanged into the wall behind him.

Danvers leaped up, jerked on the trigger, lunged in Bolt's direction.

Yancy couldn't get a shot off. Danvers blocked his view.

Bolt took careful aim, squeezed the trigger just as Yancy stepped out from behind the older man.

Danvers shot again as the bullet crashed into him. His hand jerked up, sending the bullet into the ceiling. Bolt's shot was at close range. It ripped through Danver's chest, exploded his heart.

Blood spurted from Danver's chest like a burst fountain. It soaked into his shirt, formed a widening crimson stain. He groaned once, slumped to the floor. His face smashed into the hard floor with a thud. His back was covered with a mass of bloody bone and sinew where the bullet had exited.

He twitched once, was dead in seconds.

Yancy glanced down at the fallen man, sick to his stomach. His pistol went slack in his hand for a brief second.

Bolt waited to see if the kid would take him on. He wouldn't kill him unless he had to.

Yancy looked away quickly. Looked back. That's as long as it took him to make up his mind. He glared at Bolt, a fierce determination in his young eyes. He brought his gun up fast, leveled it at Bolt.

He never fired the shot.

The sound of Bolt's pistol boomed in his ear.

It was the last thing he ever heard.

The bullet pierced him right between the eyes, exploded his brain, blew the back of his head away. The scream he started, ended abruptly. His hands flew to his face as his legs became rubber. He crumpled to the floor, landed on top of Danver's body.

The two men lay in a heap, a pool of blood beneath them. Bits of flesh and brain matter covered the floor, clung to the wall.

Bolt heard the footsteps coming down the hall.

The desk clerk was the first one to reach him.

"It was a fair fight," Bolt said simply.

Other men rushed up, curious to see who had been shot.

Carter checked the bodies, knew that Bolt was right. Danver's pistol was still gripped in stiffening fingers. The kid's gun was on the floor, close to the bodies. It was plain that both men had been shot from the front.

Bolt turned away, opened the door to his room.

Ginny was still huddled behind the bed. Her eyes widened when she saw him. She leaped up and ran into his arms.

"Oh, thank God you're alive," she said. "I thought . . ."

"It's all right now." He held her close to him for a

167

long time.

Two men were dead.

And it wasn't even noon.

####### *

"You ready, Elizabeth?" Horner paced his study. He hated to be kept waiting.

"Just about, Major. I'll be down in a minute."

"Hurry up. It's almost noon."

Betsy knew she was stalling. She sat at her dressing table, brushing her hair to a sheen. She was already dressed but she wanted a few more minutes to herself before they rode into town to meet her father. She wore her favorite outfit, a long pink skirt with a matching jacket that buttoned up the front. She wore a sheer pink blouse under the jacket. It was simple, but comfortable and she knew she looked good in it. She wanted to look nice when she met her father.

That was why she was stalling. She was nervous about seeing her father again. Her stomach twisted into knots every time she thought about what her father would say to Major when the two met for the first time. It could be very uncomfortable if her father started talking about her previous encounter with Bolt.

Maybe she was worrying over nothing. She should give her father more credit than she did. He would have more sense than to mention the brief affair she'd had with Bolt before she married Horner.

Luke Scarnes was the problem. It was clear to her that Luke hadn't run to Major about his news about her and Bolt. But he still held that over her head.

168

Betsy looked in the mirror, gave her face a final scrutiny, dabbed toilet water behind her ears. It wouldn't do to wait any longer.

She walked down the stairway, lifting her skirt so she wouldn't trip over it.

"I'm ready, Major."

"Good. The buggy's hitched up." He came out of his study to meet her. "You look lovely, Elizabeth."

"Thanks. I don't know where we're supposed to meet my father. He didn't say in his letter."

"You worry about things too much," he laughed. "The town's not that big. We'll find him."

****

"I think I'd better get back and check on Belle," said Ginny.

"I'll go with you." Bolt opened the door, looked out in the hallway. The bodies of Danvers and Yancy had been taken away. A young man with a bucket of soapy water was scrubbing the floor with a scrub brush. A bottle of carbolic acid stood near the wall. The floor smelled of lye.

They walked back across the street to the Cherokee Hotel.

When they got to Belle's room, she looked up and smiled. Her eyes were dull, listless.

"Not feeling any better?" Bolt asked.

"Not much."

Bolt reached over and felt her cheeks, her forehead.

"You've got a fever," he said. "Do you want to see the doctor?"

"No, I'll be all right if I can get some rest."

169

"Ginny, I think you better take her out to the ranch and take care of her." He turned to Belle. "Think you can ride that far?"

"Sure, I could, but I think I'd better stay here."

"You'll be safer out at the ranch. A lot's going on in town and I don't want you staying here."

"But we'll have to come back in to go to work in a few hours anyway."

"You're not going to work tonight. Either one of you. You're sick, Belle. You need to take care of yourself."

"But it's Friday. That's one of our busiest nights at the Panhandle Club," she protested.

"It doesn't matter. They can get along without you for a night or two."

"He's right," said Ginny. "We could both use some time off. Come on, I'll take you home and nurse you back to health. I'll make some soup."

"You'd better stop at the store and get her some medicine," he told Ginny.

"I've got some tonic at home."

"Good. I'll stop by the Panhandle Club and tell your boss you won't be in for a couple of days."

Ginny helped Belle out of bed.

"Guess I'm weaker than I thought," she said when she stood up.

"Are you sure you can make it?"

"Yes. I'll feel better when I get in my own bed."

"I'll be out later. Take care."

Bolt left the room, walked outside, headed toward the Panhandle Club.

****

170

The lean man rode into town, his pistol tied low on his leg.

Ed Kendrick was a stranger to Black Mesa.

He wouldn't be here long. Wouldn't stay the night if he was lucky. He'd take care of business, then move on.

Kendrick halted his horse in front of the meat market which was right in the middle of the town. He wasn't sure where he was going, so this was just as good a place to tie up as any.

He climbed down from his saddle, weary from the long days on the trail. He looped the reins over the hitchrail, pulled them tight, stepped back. He removed his Stetson, whacked it across his pant leg to shake loose the trail dust, then slipped it back on his head.

Kendrick looked up just as Bolt was approaching the Panhandle Club across the street. He squinted his eyes to narrow slits, saw Bolt enter the saloon.

Bolt had not looked his way.

Kendrick smiled.

Bolt was not the only person he was looking for, though. There were three other people in Black Mesa he was interested in. One of them, the man who had hired him, would look him up while he was there, pay him for doing the job he'd come to do.

Kendrick kicked his boots against the hitchrail. Caked-on dirt crumbled, fell to the ground. He fumbled in his pocket for the makings, built himself a quirly.

The boards creaked as he ambled along the boardwalk, stopped in front of the mercantile store. The smoke from his cigarette drifted away from him as he leaned against the wall. He studied the town, the people who came and went.

He'd seen plenty of small towns in his time. The people were always the same. They shopped at markets and cried at funerals. Some went to barbershops, some went to church. Some ran businesses while others ran the town. There were women with babies, glitter gals with gaudy dresses. Men who worked and got nowhere, others who did nothing and prospered. It was the same in all towns. And, always, there were those who killed.

His eyes drifted back to the Panhandle Club as the batwing doors swung open. He saw Bolt step out into the bright sunlight, head his way. Kendrick dropped his cigarette to the ground, stomped on it with his boot. He touched his fingers to the brim of his Stetson, pulled it down slightly to conceal his face.

As Bolt got closer, Kendrick turned around slowly, his back to the street. He studied the displays in the store window until Bolt had gone on by him. He turned around, pushed his hat back with one finger. He watched Bolt walk down the street, past several falsefronts and finally turn in at the livery stable.

Kendrick could take care of his business right then if he had a mind to. But he wouldn't. He wanted to see his daughter first, meet her husband.

The pimp would have to wait.

Kendrick was smoking another cigarette when he saw the horse and buggy approaching from the other end of town. He recognized the woman in it from a block away. The long blonde hair blowing in the breeze was not hard to spot.

He waited until the buggy was almost in front of

172

him before he stepped out in the street, waved his hands.

"Father!" Betsy shrieked when she spotted him.

Horner reined up on the horse, brought it to a halt in front of the store. While Major tied the horse to a post, Kendrick walked over, helped his daughter down from the buggy.

Betsy threw her arms around her father's neck, hugged him. The sight of him after so long made her forget her worries.

"Oh, Father, it's so good to see you."

Kendrick stepped back, held her hand.

"You're looking well, Elizabeth. As beautiful as ever."

"You always say that."

She flipped her hand in the air. She turned her head, saw Major standing next to her, waiting while she greeted her father.

"Father, this is my husband, Major."

Horner stuck out a ham hock of a hand. Kendrick shook it with a firm grip.

Major was surprised at Kendrick's appearance. He had expected him to be a handsome, dignified man with graying hair, a middle-aged paunch, perhaps. He was anything but that. Kendrick was a whip-lean man, almost cadaverous, with a hard chiseled face, thin, cruel lips. He wore his dark hair long, shabby.

Kendrick was equally startled by Horner's size, his massive frame. He felt an instant dislike for the man. He'd known men like Horner before, men who used their size to bully their way through life. They used people to get what they wanted, to do their dirty work. He wondered if Elizabeth was anything more than a showpiece for Horner's ego. Probably not. He hoped he was wrong for Elizabeth's sake.

Elizabeth was the only thing that really mattered to Kendrick. He'd raised her by himself and wanted the very best for her. That's why he'd been critical of the boys who had courted her. That's why he'd pushed her into a career of teaching school. It was respectable.

Kendrick had no ties anymore. No place he could call home. Not since Elizabeth left. He went where he was needed. Where men would pay his price to do what he did best. That was why he was in Black Mesa. He would get his price.

"Let's go eat," said Kendrick. "I hope there's a place where we can get a good steak."

"Andersons has the best food, don't you think, Elizabeth?" said Horner.

"Yes."

Horner took charge, waved his massive arm in the air, pointed to their left. "It's just down the street."

They entered the small cafe that didn't display its name. The only sign in the window proclaimed, "Good home cooking." Mrs. Anderson escorted them to a table on one side of the small room, handed them a hand-printed menu. Horner pulled out a chair, held it for Elizabeth. Kendrick sat across from them, his back to the door. When Mrs. Anderson came back a few minutes later to take their order, Horner ordered a special wine to go with their meal.

Kendrick looked at his daughter, smiled. She looked exactly like her mother had when she died giving birth to Elizabeth.

"What brings you to Black Mesa, Father?"

"Just passing through. On my way to Dodge City."

"I hope you'll come out to the ranch and spend a few days with us."

"Won't be here that long."

She was disappointed.

"Surely you'll stay one night."

"Don't think so."

She knew it wouldn't do any good to beg. Her father had always been like that. She remembered the times when she was growing up when her father went out of town on business, times when she desperately wanted him to stay home. Like the time she sang a solo in the school Christmas pageant. All the other children in the pageant had their parents there. She had only Mrs. Greenwald, who took care of her when her father was gone.

Sometimes she felt she barely knew her father. She didn't even know how he earned his money. He told her that he was a drover, and she didn't doubt that he'd done that at some time. But the last few years he'd been evasive about his trips out of town. There was always plenty of money around and when she got older, she realized that there wasn't that kind of money in driving cattle.

Mrs. Anderson came through the kitchen door, balancing three plates in her hands. She had already served the wine, the wine glasses. She set the plates on the table.

"Enjoy your meal," she said.

Kendrick dug into the steak, ravenous. He had kept his meals to a minimum on the trail. Black coffee for breakfast, beef jerky and hardtack for lunch. It was only when he stopped in a town for lodging that he indulged in a big meal.

He held a fork in his hand, used a biscuit to push the potatoes onto the fork. He looked at his daughter, saw something in her eyes that disturbed him. A sadness, a fear. He swallowed the bite of food, looked Horner square in the eyes.

"You able to keep my daughter happy, Major?"

The question took Horner by surprise. He cursed under his breath. Kendrick should have asked Elizabeth if she'd been able to keep him happy, see her reaction. Not lately, she hadn't. She'd been cold as a dead fish for the last couple of weeks.

"Yes, I think so." Horner forced a smile, put his arm around his wife.

"That true, Elizabeth?" He dabbed the biscuit into the gravy, shoved it in his mouth.

"Father!" There it was again. Her father interfering with her life. She supposed he was just concerned with her welfare, but she didn't like it. It was rude. "Yes . . . of course," she muttered. She couldn't look her father in the eyes. She cringed, toyed with her food.

Luke Scarnes came through the front door, headed toward Horner's table. Betsy looked up, saw him coming. Her stomach twisted in knots, her throat went dry. She held her breath, looked down at her plate, prayed that he wouldn't say anything he shouldn't.

"I gotta talk to you, Major," he said as he came up to the table. He stopped short when he saw Kendrick. His eyes widened briefly before he recovered from the surprise. He nodded politely, didn't let on that he knew the lean man.

"What is it, Luke?" Horner asked.

"Outside."

"Yes, of course." Horner scooted his chair back, lifted his hulk out of it. "By the way, this is Elizabeth's father, Ed Kendrick. Mr. Kendrick, this is my foreman, Luke Scarnes."

"Please to meet you, Mr. Scarnes." Kendrick put his fork across his plate, extended his hand. He, too, pretended that they were meeting for the first time.

"Excuse me, please," Horner said. "I'll be right back."

Betsy waited until Horner was gone before she spoke again.

"Father, you shouldn't have asked Major what you did."

"About keeping you happy? I got a right. You're my daughter, you know."

"You don't like him, do you?" she asked.

"Don't know him that well."

"Well, to put your mind at ease, he's good to me. He buys me anything I want. He's a good provider."

"That don't guarantee happiness."

"Say it straight, Father."

"I don't think he's good enough for you."

She broke into tears, exasperated by his questioning, his probing in her life. Why did she always feel the need to explain herself to him?

"What are you trying to do to me? You're going to ruin my life again. Why can't you let me live my own life?"

"I'm sorry, Elizabeth." He reached out a hand, pulled it back quickly. "I didn't mean anything

177

by it."

She dabbed at her tears with her napkin.

"I know you didn't, Father, but you're always finding something wrong with the men in my life."

There was an awkward silence between them.

"Tell me about yourself," she said, changing the subject. "What are you doing these days?"

He thought for a long moment. His eyes turned cold.

"Keep your own house," he said. "I'll keep mine."

****

Outside the cafe, Scarnes gave Horner the bad news.

"Danvers and Yancy. Both dead. The stake-out didn't work. Bolt killed 'em both."

"Sonofabitch! Can't anyone stop that man?"

"Try it if you like."

Horner's temper flared. The flush started at his neck, creeped up to his face. The veins in his neck stood out.

"Damn it, this is the last straw! Where's that man you promised to bring in? If he doesn't get here right away, I'll take Bolt out myself."

"No need," said Luke. "The man's in town. He's the best there is."

CHAPTER SEVENTEEN

"Your horse ain't quite ready, Mr. Bolt," said Billy Webster. "My daddy's been real busy this morning."

"How much longer?"

"Can't say. Daddy went home to eat his dinner. He'll be back in less than an hour. Shouldn't take him long when he gets back."

"He should have finished before he left." Bolt's tone was sharp.

"Yes, sir, Mr. Bolt." Billy didn't want to make Bolt angry. "Word's going around that you killed two men this morning. That true?"

"It's true."

"You ain't ascairt of nobody, are you, Mr. Bolt?"

"Doesn't do any good to be afraid of people, Billy. You shouldn't fear anything in your life. Be aware of things. Do what you think is right, and be careful. It's that simple."

"I hope I can be like you when I'm all growed up."

"Just be yourself, Billy, and you'll do fine."

Billy puffed out his chest, went back to graining the horses.

"When your father gets back, tell him I need my

horse right away."

"I sure will, Mr. Bolt."

"I'll be back in about an hour."

Bolt went through the door of the livery stable, stood outside for a minute.

Damn. He had a whole hour to kill. He wanted to get back to the ranch right away, check on Belle. He still had a lot of work to do out there before he was through. Maybe he could find Tom. He wanted to talk to him anyway.

It didn't take him long to find Tom. He knew the Roosters Nest was the only place in town where the glitter gals worked during the daylight hours. It was a quiet place, out of the way, a block from the main street. They didn't serve hard liquor there. Only beer. So the rowdies didn't frequent it very often.

Bolt walked a block to Front Street, turned south, walked another block. He saw the unlit lantern hanging on the sign post in front of the Roosters Nest, a two-story frame house.

The smell of heavy perfume permeated the air, hit Bolt's nostrils when he walked through the door. Scents of lilac and lavender. The room was not set up like a saloon, although there was a small bar along one wall.

Three painted ladies with skimpy, gaudy clothes sat on a long couch in the middle of the room. One of them, a striking brunette named Freida, fluffed her hair, gave Bolt a sidelong look when he walked across the room.

There were three large divans in the room, several plush overstuffed chairs, a few low tables. The room had a comfortable, homey atmosphere to it. A fire burned slowly in a stone fireplace, glowing coal oil lanterns gave the room a soft light. An expensive rug covered the main area, smaller braided throw rugs were scattered across the highly polished wood floors. Heavy velvet drapes kept the daylight out.

Tom grinned when he saw Bolt.

"What brings you to this neck of the woods?"

Tom sprawled on the red velvet couch, his feet propped up on a long low table. A girl with bright red lipstick, smudges of pink rouge on her cheeks, sat next to him, her arms hanging around his neck. Jenny's large breasts jutted out from the low cut garment she wore, pressed into Tom's side. The bottom of her green shiny outfit stopped at her thighs, just barely covered her privates. Black net stockings showed her long legs to advantage. She crossed and uncrossed her legs in a teasing fashion, nibbled on Tom's ear.

Bolt plopped down in one of the overstuffed chairs facing Tom and his playmate.

"Nothing much. Got some time on my hands. Waiting for my horse."

Bolt had just barely sat down when Freida rose from the couch, wriggled her chunky hips and came toward Bolt. She was young, still showed her baby fat. She had a pretty face, but her plump figure detracted from her looks.

She sat down on the arm of Bolt's chair, wrapped an arm around his neck. She peppered him with short kisses on the cheek, forehead, neck. She ran her hand across his trousers, groped for his bulge.

"Hello, good looking," she said, pursing her lips to a small circle. "Want to have some fun?"

Bolt politely untangled himself from her clutches, leaned forward.

"Not right now, sweetheart. I got business with my friend here."

Tom sat up, laughed heartily as Bolt turned down the zealous wanton. Freida flipped her dark hair back, pouted, walked back to the couch to wait with the other girls for a more promising customer.

"You got time to talk, Tom?"

"Sure." He turned to Jenny, gave her a quick kiss on the mouth. "Would you mind, sweetie?"

"If you're not too long," she drawled, the honey dripping from her words. "Your baby can't wait much longer." She reached over, tweaked his knob, then got up. "I'll go on upstairs and wait for you. Room twenty-two."

"I'll find you."

"Come on, Tom, I'll buy you a beer."

Tom got up, followed Bolt to the small bar. Two young men sitting at the far end of the bar were flanked by two glitter gals making their pitch.

"For a minute, I thought you were actually going to shell out money for a woman's pleasures," Tom laughed.

"Hell no. You won't ever find me paying for it."

"What the hell you got against whores?"

"Nothing. I just don't believe in paying for what you can get for nothing."

"It's a damn sight easier doing it my way," said Tom. "You always form attachments with your women."

"And that's bad?"

"Not always. But you always get so involved with

them that you get yourself into a whole kettle of trouble trying to help them out. Like with Belle. You try to do a favor for an old girlfriend and look what it's got you."

"I never turn a lady down when she needs me."

They stopped talking while the bartender served their beers. Tom looked at his friend for a long moment.

"You think you're too good for the glitter gals?"

Bolt was irritated by Tom's remark.

"You know better than that, Tom. Otherwise I wouldn't run two whorehouses. I treat them damn decent."

"But you never sleep with any of the girls who work for you."

"It's not because I don't like them. That's a business. It would just complicate matters. It would cause problems, jealousies, if I had a favorite."

"There are already jealousies. They're jealous of you and Cassie."

"That's different. Cassie isn't a prostitute. She runs the place for me when I'm gone."

"That proves my point. You do think you're too good for whores."

Bolt gave a big sigh.

"Tom, you don't understand. I think prostitutes are basically better than other women. They're honest about what they do. They're not afraid to show their sexuality. They don't pull that phony coy, shy shit on you. You know where you stand with them. I can't stand the society women who put on the airs, the ones who think their shit don't stink. Well, it does, just like yours and mine and everybody else's.

I hate women who cry and whine to get their way. The possessive ones are the worst. They cling to you like a smothering vine and then they throw a big fit if they find out you did the same thing to another woman that you did to them."

"Then why do you get involved with women like that?"

"It's my way of learning about people, I guess. Another thing, it's good to have a close relationship, even if it's brief."

"You ought to try it once. Freida's not that bad."

"A little plump for me."

"Aw, the better to bounce on, my friend."

"Tom, I'll bet you've tried out every whore in town."

"Not quite. I've missed a few. You've kept me too busy. Did you come here to shoot the shit or you got something on your mind?"

"They're closing in on me. Did you hear about the shootings this morning?"

"No. Haven't been anyplace but here since I got to town."

"It figures."

"Who got shot?"

"Two of Horner's best guns. They had me staked out. He's gonna run out of men if it keeps up."

"The bastard's got no balls or he'd come after you himself."

"He won't be too happy about losing Danvers and Yancy. He'll try to get even. Man like that doesn't know when to give up."

"I don't know why that land's so damned important to him."

"It's good land, but it's more than that. He thinks he's got a lot of power. He thinks he can snap his finger, pay a price and get what he wants. He's determined to get Belle and Ginny's land, no matter what the cost."

"It probably makes him even madder that he can't just buy off two measly gals."

"That's the whole thing. Men think a woman's got her place and she should stay there. They think women should stay at home and be wives and mothers, or old maid school teachers. Or whores. Men don't cotton to women who want to start their own business and get ahead in this world. Horner can't stand it that Belle and Ginny could be successful raising cattle. They've got better land than he does because of the river. There's a chance they can do better than he can. Wipe him out. It's a threat to his manhood."

"Why don't you take him out? Settle things in a hurry?"

"Because it's his problem. He's the one who has to live with it. He'll fail on his own. I want him to live to see it."

"Makes about as much sense as a mud bath."

"It'll hit you sometime, Tom." Bolt sipped on the beer. "I got a favor to ask."

"I know your favors, Bolt," Tom grinned. "Think I'll pass."

"When you get through with your fun and games here, would you go on back to the ranch? Belle's sick and Ginny took her home. I told them I'd be out later, but I think I'll stick around town. See if I can't draw Horner out. Bring this thing to a head. I don't trust him or any of his men, especially if they find out the girls are alone out there. I'd feel better if you were there."

"Yeah. I'll ride on out when I finish my business here."

"Don't be all day."

"Shouldn't take more than an hour or two."

"Think you're man enough to last that long?" Bolt laughed.

Bolt left the Roosters Nest to pick up his horse. After he did that, he'd stop at the store, buy an extra rifle, fresh ammunition. He'd find a place to stash it in his room at the Cimarron. He never again wanted to be caught without a spare weapon like he had that morning.

****

Tom finished his beer before he left the bar. When he walked across the room, to the stairway, the girls on the couch began smiling at him, taunting him.

"I'll show you a good time, mister," called the one in red.

"Come to my room," said Freida, thrusting her tits out, rubbing her thighs suggestively.

"Sorry, girls," Tom smiled. "I've got someone waiting for me."

"Jenny?" said the third one. "She's probably fallen asleep waiting for you."

"You man enough to take us all on?" teased one.

"Some other time," said Tom as he went up the staircase and disappeared.

He walked down the hall, tapped on the door of

room twenty-two.

"Come on in, the door's unlocked."

Penrod opened the door, stepped inside. The bed was turned down, but he didn't see Jenny.

She waited behind the door, completely naked. When he was inside the room, she made her move. She came up behind him, pressed her bare breasts into his back, reached around his hips and grabbed his crotch.

"Guess who?" she said.

"Who cares. Just don't stop." He whirled her around, kissed her passionately.

She insisted on undressing him, which she did quickly after locking the door. She led him to the bed, pushed him down on the fresh sheets.

A minute later she was all over him, sprinkling kisses all over his body. They felt like tiny bee stings.

Neither of them heard the noise at the door a half hour later as someone tried the doorknob. Jenny had played with him all that time, making him so excited he couldn't wait any longer. Tom had just rolled over on her, penetrated her.

The door splintered with a loud thud as the intruder burst through.

"What the hell?" yelled Tom.

Tom rolled off her, reached above him for his pistol.

It wasn't there. It was under the heap of clothes on the floor near the door.

Jenny brought the sheet up around her chin, stayed where she was.

It was Luke Scarnes.

Tom was staring down the barrel of a .45.

Scarnes was backed up by two other gunnies. J. D. Walters and the kid, Sammy Recher. Walter's Colt was drawn. Sammy had a Winchester rifle in the crook of his arm.

"Come on, lover boy, you're going with us," barked Scarnes.

Tom looked around, saw that there was no way to escape. They'd nail him if he tried it.

"Aw shit," Tom drawled. "Can't you fellers see I'm busy?"

"Get a move on, smart ass." Scarnes jabbed his pistol in Tom's direction.

Tom stood by the bed, stark naked, his manhood shriveled up to a limp mass of flesh. There was a slim chance. If he could only reach his pistol.

"Mind if I get dressed first?" Tom asked, eyeing the heap of clothes. The pistol, holster were underneath the clothes, hidden from view.

"Make it snappy." Luke kicked at the clothes, sent them scooting across the floor toward Tom. As soon as he did it, he realized there was something heavier than clothes in the pile.

Tom leaned over, reached for the clothes, hoped to conceal his weapon long enough to slip it out of the holster.

The toe of Luke's boot came crashing down on Tom's hand. The pistol scooted a foot away. Luke picked it up, kept his eyes on Tom.

Tom jerked his hand back, squeezed it with his other hand for a second. He drew back his arm, made a fist.

"Try it and you'll draw back a bloody stump," said Scarnes. "Now get your clothes on. I'm tired of looking at your puny body."

Jenny saw Sammy leering at her, pulled the covers tighter around her throat.

Tom took his time putting his clothes on. He was stalling for time.

Luke shoved the gun against Tom's ribs, pulled the hammer back. "Move it," he ordered.

Tom finished dressing, thought about bringing his boot down on Scarnes' pistol hand. He changed his mind when the other two men took a step closer, waved their weapons menacingly.

Scarnes moved around behind Tom, stuck the pistol at Tom's back.

"Come on," Scarnes ordered, jabbing the pistol at Tom for emphasis. "We're going for a long ride."

"Where we going?" asked Tom.

"You'll know soon enough."

Tom looked over at Jenny.

"Sorry, baby. I owe you one."

CHAPTER EIGHTEEN

Scarnes walked directly behind Tom, down the stairs, through the large room below. He kept his pistol snugged up against Tom's back. J. D. and Sammy were right behind them.

The women huddled in a corner of the room, watched the procession with wide eyes. The two men who had been at the bar were gone.

Outside, Scarnes ordered Tom to get on his horse. Tom balked, stood his ground.

"Don't stall anymore, Penrod," said Scarnes. "I'd just as soon blast you away now as later."

Tom took his time climbing into the saddle. He wasn't going to make it easy for them.

Scarnes waited until J. D. and Sammy had mounted their horses and had Tom covered before he swung himself up on his own horse.

"J. D., come around here, on this side of Penrod," ordered Scarnes. "Sammy, I want you to ride on the other side. You're gonna lead this parade, Penrod. Turn right at the corner. Stay off the main street. When you get to the edge of town, head for the Rocking H. Keep your horse at a nice easy pace. No fast riding. No fancy tricks. Just keep your eyes straight ahead and you won't get hurt. And don't forget, I'll be right behind you. Try anything and you'll be pushing up daisies.''

Tom touched his boots to his horse's flanks. The mare reared its head, moved forward slowly. Tom followed Scarnes' directions, stayed away from the busy main street. When they got away from the town, Tom searched desperately for a chance to outsmart his kidnappers. If they dropped their guard for even a minute, he would try to escape. So far, they stuck to him like glue.

He kept his head straight, but his eyes darted back and forth as he kept track of the two men who rode beside him. He saw Sammy relax his grip on the rifle, saw the rifle gradually lower, the long barrel point downward. It was now or never.

Tom threw himself forward so he was flat against the horse's neck. At the same instant, he kicked the horse in the flanks. The mare bolted forward, took off at a gallop.

Sammy's rifle came up fast. He didn't shoot. Instead he spurred his horse at the same time J. D. kicked his.

Tom didn't have a chance to gain enough distance to escape. A minute later the two men overtook him. They ran their horses around in front of Tom, slowing his horse.

Scarnes rode up beside them, grabbed the rifle from Sammy's hands.

"That was real funny," snarled Scarnes as he jabbed the rifle butt into Tom's ribs. "Care to try it again?"

Tom winced with the pain.

"Get moving," ordered Scarnes.

Tom hunched in the saddle, favoring his side. He didn't try it again. The Rocking H Ranch loomed up ahead of them.

When they rode up to the ranch, Scarnes told J. D. and Sammy to take Penrod into the bunkhouse, tie him up.

"Stay with him," he said. "See that he don't try to break his hobbles."

Luke found Major in the livingroom. Elizabeth was with him. Luke wished Horner was alone.

"Ah, there you are, Luke. I've been looking for you. Have you got anything to report yet?"

Luke glared at Betsy as he walked past her.

"If you mean has my man taken care of his business yet, no, not yet. Give him a chance."

Betsy's sigh of relief was barely audible, but Luke heard it. She knew what they were talking about, even if Luke was trying to talk in code.

Luke shot her a hard, threatening look.

"But I brought you a present," Luke told Major.

"Huh?"

"Yeah, I brought in Bolt's partner, Tom Penrod. He's tied up out in the bunkhouse."

"Why'd you do a damned fool thing like that? I don't want Penrod. I want Bolt."

"I didn't want Penrod to get in the way of our man."

"If your man's as good as you say he is, he doesn't need any help from you." Horner's remark was meant to be sarcastic.

Betsy got up from the couch, walked over to the

two men.

"Major, this is all so pointless. All these killings. You don't need that land. Let the VeeBee girls have their ranch. There's plenty of other property around here. Please put a stop to all this bloodshed. Don't have any more men killed. No land is worth the price of human lives."

"I want that land, Elizabeth," Horner said, "and I'm going to get it."

"Please, Major, I beg you, stop these killings now. Be a man. A real man. Don't get your own success at the expense of others. If you do nothing else in your life, show that you're bigger than anyone else. Stop the murders. If you care anything about me."

Horner paced the floor, chomping on an unlit cigar. She had stabbed him with her words. He didn't like her talking that way in front of Luke.

Luke didn't like the way things were going. He showed his displeasure by glaring at her.

Horner walked up to his wife.

"I'm sorry, Elizabeth. It has to be my way," he told her.

She was desperate. Her pleading wasn't working. Her anger flared up until she could no longer control it.

"What kind of a man are you, Major? Are you so afraid that two women might make a go of a cattle ranch that you'd resort to this?"

"Elizabeth, enough," he warned.

Luke backed away, watched them quarrel, gloating inside.

"I won't be quiet about this," she continued. "I used to think you were the most perfect man in the

193

world. You've been successful and wealthy all your life. Now I know how you got your money. By using other people, destroying them. Now you've stooped to the lowest form of existence. Trying to destroy two women. It doesn't bother you at all that your men have been killed. Just because you're greedy. You've used your own men, allowed their lives to be taken from them just so you can get what you want. You're . . . you're . . ."

"That's enough, Elizabeth!" He struggled to control his temper.

"I haven't finished! You don't risk your own life. Only your men. Where's your pride?"

"Elizabeth, I'm sorry about the men who have died."

"You don't give a damn about anybody but yourself. You don't even care about me."

"That's not true."

"Yes it is. You don't take the time to make me happy. You're too busy with your own greed. You've used me the same as you have the others."

He wanted to slap her face. He probably would have if Luke hadn't been there.

"You'll never change," she continued. "I'm sick of hearing about the cattle empire you want. It's cost too many lives already. You've ordered someone to kill Bolt. It won't end there, either. You'll keep killing." She broke into tears, covered her face with her hands.

Luke saw the marriage crumbling before his eyes. He had the power to push it along. He swaggered over to Horner.

"I've got something I think you should know," Luke said smugly. He glanced at Elizabeth, a smirk

194

on his face.

"Not now, Luke."

"I think you ought to hear me out. It can't wait."

"What is it?" Horner snapped.

"You want to know why Elizabeth's carrying on like she is?"

"Say it straight. And say it fast."

"She ain't been exactly faithful to you."

A gasp escaped Elizabeth's lips.

"She's got herself a lover." Luke was playing both sides against the middle.

Horner was stunned. It took a few seconds for Luke's words to sink in. He couldn't believe what he was hearing. Elizabeth had always been faithful. He was sure of it.

"Can you guess who her lover is?" taunted Luke.

Horner stood there, speechless.

"Bolt! She's been sleeping with him."

There was hatred in his eyes when Major looked at his wife.

"Is that true, Elizabeth?" He clenched his fists.

She shrank back away from him, suddenly afraid of her husband. She opened her mouth, was too scared to speak.

"Answer me, Elizabeth!"

"She can't deny it," prodded Luke. "She's even been over to the VeeBee Ranch to play house with him."

"Shut up, Luke!"

"Tell him about the hotel room, Elizabeth, where you and Bolt made love for hours."

"He'd better be lying to me," Horner said, stepping closer to Betsy.

"He . . . he . . ."

"You'd better tell me the truth, woman. Did you sleep with Bolt?"

"Yes!" she blurted.

"That's why she was begging you not to kill Bolt," Luke said. "She didn't want to lose her lover."

Luke's words sent Horner over the edge. He became insane with rage, with jealousy.

"How could you, you little tramp?"

"It . . . it just happened."

"Just happened, my ass. You'd better tell me the truth right now," he threatened. "Did Bolt force you . . . ?"

"No, he didn't force me."

"You mean you were willing?"

"It just happened, I told you."

"You filthy whore!" He slapped her hard across the face. A red welt marred her face, swelling the skin.

"You faithless bitch!" He slapped her again, across the mouth. Blood trickled from her split lip. She ran her tongue across the cut, tasted the warm blood. Tears blinded her.

He came at her again, landed a blow across her ear.

Her hands flew to her head. She cupped her ear, put the other one over her mouth.

"Don't, Major. Don't hit me anymore."

He brought his monstrous hand up again.

She raised her arms in front of her face, tried to ward off another blow.

He pushed her hard, sent her sprawling to the floor.

"Leave me alone, you louse!" she shouted.

He kicked her on the shin.

"Get up!"

"Get away from me!" she sobbed.

He reached down, grabbed her by the hair, pulled her to a standing position.

"You'll be sorry for this!" he boomed.

"You're insane!"

"You'll see how insane I am."

He smacked a fist into her eye. She reeled backwards.

"Stop, Major! Please stop."

"You're gonna pay dearly for sleeping with that bastard Bolt! I'll kill you!"

He swung his arm, whacked her across the shoulder. The glancing blow sent her whirling. He lashed out with the other arm, missed her. She fell, landed on the couch. He followed her, started pounding on her back, her head.

Luke stepped in. He'd gotten the reaction he wanted, but he hadn't expected Horner to become so violent. He knew that Horner's rage had made him crazy, that the man didn't know what he was doing.

"Stop it, Horner! You're gonna kill her."

"Yes, I am."

Luke tugged at Horner's shoulders. Horner resisted. His rage made him stronger than usual.

Horner brought his arm back to strike his wife again. Luke caught the arm, twisted it enough to force Horner back a little. Quickly, Luke stepped in between, managed to push Horner away. He kept shoving with all his strength until Major was a safe distance from Elizabeth.

"Calm down, Major. You don't know what you're doing."

Horner took a deep breath, clenched his fists. His breath came in short gasps. He closed his eyes.

Luke placed his hand on Horner's shoulder. "Get a grip on yourself."

Gradually, Horner's breathing returned to normal. He looked over at his wife who was huddled on the couch, deep sobs wracking her body.

"My God, what have I done to you?" He brought his hands up to his face, covered his eyes, bent his head down. He began to weep.

"It's over with, Major," Luke said. "You didn't know what you were doing." He let Luke lead him into his study, where he collapsed in his chair, cradled his head in his arms and began to weep.

In the livingroom, Betsy slowly picked herself up off the couch, went up the stairs, clutching the railing for support. She sat down in front of the mirror.

It was a long time before she could look at herself. She was shocked when she saw her reflection. She didn't even recognize herself.

She knew she could never live with her husband again. She had lost the last shred of respect for him. She hated him for what he had done to her.

She had to leave now. Before it was too late. Before she became trapped again in a marriage that had turned sour.

She went to the dresser, poured water from the porcelain pitcher into the matching bowl. Gingerly, she dabbed at her face, washing away the dried blood. She held the washcloth against her eye. She changed into a clean dress, brushed her hair. It was all she could do.

She took nothing with her when she left except her horse.

CHAPTER NINETEEN

Bolt placed the Winchester under the mattress in his room at the hotel. He let the mattress back down, smoothed the covers. It wasn't the best hiding place, but at least it didn't create a tell-tale bulge. There was no other place to hide it in the small barren room.

He was just ready to leave when someone rapped lightly on the door. From habit, he whipped out his pistol, had it cocked as he cleared leather. He froze where he was, waited, listened.

The tap came again.

"Who is it?" he called.

"It's me, Betsy. Let me in."

He unlocked the door, opened it slowly. He jumped to the other side of the door, his back against the wall, kicked the door wide open with his boot.

Betsy stepped inside. Bolt stuck his head out the door, checked the hallway. He closed the door, locked it.

"Howdy . . ." That's when he saw her face. "What happened to you?" He looked closer, was repulsed by the sight.

"Major beat me up. Almost killed me."

"How come?"

"He found out about us . . ."

"How?"

"Luke Scarnes told him."

"Now we know who followed you over to the VeeBee that day."

"Yes."

"Anything broken?"

"I don't think so. I hurt all over."

"I'm sorry, Betsy. Real sorry. I feel like this is all my fault."

She wanted him to feel that way. Maybe he'd feel sorry enough to take her away from here.

"It was terrible. He just kept hitting me. He's got a terrible temper. I was so frightened."

"Sit down. Let me put a damp cloth on your eye."

"No, not now. I've got to leave town. I'm too scared to go back home. I didn't think Luke would tell him, but he did. Major went crazy when he found out."

Bolt's eyebrows shot up.

"You mean you knew that Luke knew about us?"

"Well, yes."

"How long have you known?"

"A couple of days, I guess."

"Why didn't you come to me when you first knew?"

"I just didn't think he'd go through with it. He said he wouldn't tell Major if I left town."

"You should have gotten away from here right then."

"I know. Bolt, will you go with me? I need you."

"I can't go. I told you that before."

"Please, Bolt. I can't make it on my own. I don't

have anyplace to go. Please."

"Take it easy, Besy. You're pretty banged up. Lie down a while." He led her to the bed, helped her lie down on it.

"Bolt, lie down next to me."

"No."

"But I need you."

"Not that way, you don't."

"Please. Just for a few minutes."

"Look, Betsy. You could rupture a blood vessel."

"At least sit down next to me."

"First I'm going to get a piece of steak to put on that eye of yours."

"Don't leave me, please."

"It'll only take a minute. I can get a beefsteak downstairs in the hotel kitchen. It will take the swelling down, give you a little relief."

"Hurry," she said.

When he returned, he placed the small slab of meat over her eye.

"That feel better?"

"Yes. Sit down," she said, patting the covers next to her.

Bolt sat down on the edge of the bed.

She winced in pain when his weight hit the bed.

"Hurts bad, doesn't it?"

"Yes. You've got to take me away someplace." She started to weep.

"Don't cry, Betsy," he pleaded. He couldn't stand a whining woman, even if she had good reason. "It's impossible for me to go with you. You'll be all right. You don't need me."

"Yes I do," she sobbed. "I don't know where to go.

What to do.''

"You can go home to your father until you get on your feet."

"I couldn't. He's here in Black Mesa anyway."

"Oh?"

"Yes. Major and I had lunch with him today. He's not staying here, though. He's just passing through on his way to Dodge City."

"Maybe you could go with him."

"No. I couldn't live with him. He's always tried to run my life. It just wouldn't work. Not even for a short time."

"You can always go to a new town. Start teaching again. You're lucky, you know. Luckier than most women in your position. You've got a good education, a job to fall back on. Teachers are always in demand and the pay is pretty decent."

"I'll probably have to," she sighed.

"It's security for you."

"I don't want security. I want you," she pouted.

"You know it can't be that way."

"If you don't go away with me, they're going to kill you. Major and Luke have hired an outside gun."

"I've heard all that before."

"It's true this time. Major won't stop at anything. You won't live unless you go with me!"

"Don't talk that way, Betsy. It won't work. I don't run away."

"I wish you'd change your mind."

"You can't leave town in the shape you're in. At least not today. You should leave as soon as possible, though. I'll check on the stage, see if there's one coming through tomorrow. Did you bring any of your things?"

"No, I left everything there. I didn't want Major to know I was leaving for good or he might have tried to stop me. I have some money I've saved. I can manage for a while, until I can get a job."

"You can't stay here either. You know that. If they start looking for you, this is the first place they'd check." He thought a minute. "Can you ride out to the VeeBee Ranch? It isn't any farther than you've already ridden. Belle and Ginny are both out there. They'll take care of you. Tom's there too. You'll be safe there."

"No. Tom's not there."

"What are you saying?"

"Tom's at our place. Luke brought him out there a little while ago. That's what Luke came to the house to tell Major. Right before the trouble started."

"Why didn't you tell me before?" Bolt's jaw hardened.

"I—I guess I forgot," she said lamely.

"How could you forget something that important?" he lashed out. "My best friend's been kidnapped and you forget all about it. Or you just don't give a damn!"

"I'm sorry, Bolt." She started to cry again.

"You're really something, Betsy. You're so damned busy feeling sorry for yourself, you can't think of anyone else!"

"Please don't, Bolt," she sobbed.

Bolt snorted.

"Where is Tom? Did you see him?"

"No. Luke said he was tied up out in the bunkhouse."

"What are they going to do with him?"

"I don't know. Luke said he wanted Tom out of the way while the hired gunman took care of you. I don't think Major liked it too much."

"Damn. Come on, Betsy, you've got to get out of here." He took the raw meat off of her eye, walked to the window, opened it and hurled the beefsteak out. "Let the dogs have a feast."

Betsy eased herself to a sitting position, tested her soreness. She was ashamed that she had been so selfish. She should have told Bolt about Tom right off instead of crying about her own fate.

"Don't worry about me," she said. "I'll be all right." She stood up, put her hand to her face to ease the pain she felt when she changed positions.

"You sure you can make it out to the ranch?"

"Yes. I'll go directly there. I . . . I really am sorry, Bolt."

"I know you are. Don't worry about leaving town right away. We'll take care of you until you feel better."

"Thanks."

Bolt reached under the mattress, withdrew his new rifle.

"Here, take this," he said. "You might need it."

"Thanks." She took the rifle, left the room.

Bolt checked his pistol. He put a sixth bullet in the chamber that he normally left empty.

He was ready.

****

It didn't take Bolt long to reach the Rocking H Ranch.

He moved his horse at a good fast clip, snapping the reins near Nick's ear when the horse slowed.

He didn't know what he'd be facing when he got there, but it didn't matter. He had to get Tom out of there before anything happened to him. He owed him that.

He was in one hell of a spot. Everything seemed to be closing in on him. Tom kidnapped. Betsy slapped around by her husband. A hired gun tracking him. Belle sick with worry. And Ginny. Yes, Ginny. He was growing too fond of her.

Maybe Tom was right. It would be a hell of a lot easier to pay for the women. Not get personally involved with them. But there was no challenge that way.

Bolt slowed his horse when he neared the Rocking H Ranch. He left the road, swung around through the brush, came out behind the buildings. He reined up. Nick's nostrils flared. His coat was wet and shiny from perspiration.

Bolt was close to the bunkhouse. Fifty yards away. There were two or three men working nearby. No one looked up. None of them noticed him.

He spotted Luke Scarnes. Recognized his scarred face. Scarnes was talking to the men, giving them orders.

Bolt wondered if one of the men was the hired gun. Not likely from the looks of them. He wondered where the professional killer was. Could be around the ranch somewhere.

A thought struck Bolt. It wasn't a pleasant thought.

This could be a trap. A set up. Maybe Horner beat Betsy up, forced her to go looking for him. Maybe he told her he'd kill her if she didn't get him to come out to the ranch. If so, the trick had worked. Maybe the gun was waiting for him inside the bunkhouse. Maybe Tom wasn't there at all.

Risky. Walking into an ambush was not a way to stay healthy.

But it was a risk he had to take.

If Tom was there, he had to get him out.

Bolt took his gun out of the holster. He jabbed his spurs into his horse's flanks, rattled the reins.

He rode in fast. Straight for the bunkhouse. Right toward the cluster of men. He caught them off guard.

Scarnes whipped his pistol out of his holster, took quick aim.

Bolt looked at the three hands, watched for the sudden movement that would signal a pistol being drawn. Out of the corner of his eye, he saw the flash of metal as Scarnes drew. He swung down off his horse.

Scarnes squeezed the trigger. The shot was high. The bullet whizzed through Bolt's hat, sent it flying in the air.

Bolt took careful aim, fired before Scarnes could get off another shot.

Bolt's bullet ripped through Scarnes' chest, tore his heart apart.

Scarnes threw up his hands as the bullet ripped into him, took two steps forward, trying to regain his balance.

Blood spurted from the wound, stained his shirt crimson. He moaned, toppled to the ground. His eyes glazed over. His body twitched once and then he was dead. Vacant eyes stared up at the afternoon sun.

Bolt looked at the other men, waited to see if any of

them would go for it. They started to scatter, backing slowly away from Bolt. No one went for his gun.

"Is my friend in there?" Bolt nodded to the bunkhouse. "Tom Penrod?"

No one answered.

Bolt studied their faces, recognized Sammy Recher.

"Is anyone going to answer me? Is Penrod in that bunkhouse?"

Still no answer.

"Maybe I'll have to force it out of you. I'll start with you, Sammy." Bolt waved his pistol in Sammy's direction, wrapped his finger around the trigger.

"Yes . . . yes. He's in there." Sammy's body shook. "He's all tied up and gagged."

"Come here, Sammy."

Sammy took a couple of steps toward Bolt.

"You're going to help me, Sammy. Over here."

Sammy inched his way closer to Bolt, shaking in his boots.

Bolt kept his pistol leveled at Sammy's gut.

"Any of you foolish enough to try it," Bolt warned the other two, "you catch a bullet between the eyes."

Bolt nudged Sammy over to the door of the bunkhouse with the barrel of his pistol.

"Get in there and untie my friend. Don't try anything. I'll be right here waiting for you."

Bolt stepped into the doorway, stood facing the other two men. He moved his pistol from one to the other, kept a close eye on them.

A couple of minutes later, Tom came to the door, rubbing his wrists. He grinned at Bolt.

"Come on out here, Sammy," Bolt called.

Sammy appeared.

"You got a pistol on you?" Bolt asked Sammy.

"No, sir. I don't." Sammy's voice was quavering.

"Get me Scarnes' gun. Bring it over here."

Sammy walked over, picked Luke's gun off the ground, brought it back and handed it to Bolt, butt end first.

"Thanks, Sammy. You're a good boy."

Bolt handed the pistol to Tom. "Here, you might need this before we're through. Is your horse here?"

"Someplace. I rode it out."

"Sammy, go find Tom's horse. Bring it here."

Sammy started to leave, looked up and saw Major Horner walking from the house to the bunkhouse.

Bolt glanced up to see what Sammy was looking at.

So did the other two men.

Bolt saw the giant man crossing the yard, a rifle clutched in his hands.

"Hurry, Sammy. You make one false move and I shoot your boss."

Sammy dashed off toward the corral.

Bolt waited until the big man was closer before he spoke.

"You gonna try it, Horner?"

Horner raised the rifle, took aim.

Bolt's pistol was leveled at Horner's face.

"You do and we both die," Bolt threatened.

Horner's rifle wavered. He looked down at his dead foreman. He thought about it, knew Bolt was right. He wouldn't stand a chance against Bolt's gun. He lowered the rifle.

Bolt kept his finger wrapped around the trigger.

"I'd like to watch you squirm," said Bolt. "Die a slow, painful death." His pistol shot straight out in front of him as Bolt pointed it right between Horner's eyes.

"It doesn't matter if you kill me," Horner said calmly. "You won't survive. There's someone in town who's waiting for you, Bolt. I don't even know who it is. Luke was the only one who knew him. Now that Luke is dead, no one else knows who he is. The man has his orders. No one can stop him now."

Bolt swallowed.

Horner wasn't lying.

CHAPTER TWENTY

"I'm not going to kill you, Horner. You're not worth wasting a bullet on. You've got the blood of too many men on your hands. Good men."

"I didn't kill them, Bolt. You did."

"Because you weren't man enough to come after me yourself. Because of your greed. The deaths were senseless, needless. But you pushed your men. You tried to push Belle and Ginny, too. Only they wouldn't be pushed. What you did to your wife was brutal, inhuman. Well, you're through here, Horner. You're through pushing. You've lost everything. Your wife, your best men. Most important, you've lost your pride."

Bolt paused, let his words sink in.

"But you're not going to stay in Black Mesa," he continued. "You've got twenty-four hours to pack up and get out of town. If you're still here when we get back, I'll thrash you within an inch of your life. You'll wish you were dead."

Bolt turned to Tom.

"Come on, Tom, let's get out of here. The stench is making me sick."

Tom took the reins of his horse from Sammy who stood a few feet away, watching his boss being humiliated. He put his foot in the stirrup, drew himself up into the saddle.

Bolt walked over to where he had left his horse, mounted.

Bolt and Tom rode slowly away from the bunkhouse, away from a dead man, another who had lost everything but life itself, away from other men who were too stunned to react.

Bolt was not afraid to turn his back on these men. Horner would not shoot him. The others would not act without an order from their boss.

When they got to the dirt road, out of sight of the ranch house, Bolt held up his hand.

"Hold up a minute," he said.

Tom pulled up beside him.

Bolt slid his pistol out of the holster, fished in his pocket and drew out a bullet. He reloaded his pistol, checked it.

"Thanks for coming for me," Tom said.

"Nothing to it."

"Luke sure picked the wrong time to kidnap me," said Tom.

"Why? Did he catch you in bed?" Bolt grinned.

"Yair. Just when I was ready to . . ."

"Yeah, I know. Spare me the details."

"I'm going back into town and, uh, complete what I started. Want to go with me?"

"No. I got business of my own to take care of. I want you to go straight to the ranch. This thing isn't over yet and the girls are alone out there."

"Now? But Jenny's . . ."

"She'll have to wait. I'd go out there myself if I could. But you heard Horner. There's a man waiting for me in town. I'm going to keep that appointment."

"Be careful."

"I will. You, too. You'll be alone with three girls."

"Three?"

"Yeah. Betsy's out there too."

"How come?"

Bolt told him.

"How come he beat on her?" Tom asked.

"It's a long story. Sometime when you've got the time . . ."

"You better change your ways, Bolt," Tom grinned. "Start paying for your women and you'll save yourself a lot of trouble."

"You know, I think you might have a point there."

****

The three girls pounced on Tom when he walked into the house. They were all talking at once, surrounding him.

"Where's Bolt?" asked Ginny.

"Is he still alive?" asked Belle.

"Is he dead?" asked Betsy.

Tom threw his arms up in the air.

"Hey, slow down," he said. "One question at a time."

"What about Bolt, Tom?" said Belle. "Is he all right?"

Tom saw Betsy's banged up face.

"You look terrible," he told her.

212

"Thanks a lot," said Betsy.

"Bolt is on his way to town. There's a man waiting for him there. I sure as hell hope he makes it back."

"Oh, no," cried Betsy. "I begged him to go away from this evil town. I told him he was going to get killed." Betsy was hysterical.

"Who's the man?" asked Belle.

"Nobody knows. It's someone Luke Scarnes brought in from the outside. A professional killer."

"You mean Bolt doesn't know who he's facing?" said Ginny.

"No, Bolt doesn't know either."

"Then he's in real trouble," said Ginny.

"He's going to get killed," Betsy screamed. "He's going to die. I just know he is. Oh, why didn't he leave?"

Belle put her arms around Betsy's shoulder, tried to calm her down. "He'll be all right," Belle said. "Bolt's pretty tough."

"Bolt said you were sick, Belle," Tom said.

"I'm better, but I'm really worried about Bolt now. If he knew someone was waiting for him, why did he have to go to town? That's stupid. He could have hidden out, or hit the trail for another town."

"Bolt doesn't run away," Tom explained. "He had to face the man. Don't you understand?"

"I do," said Ginny quietly. "Can we help him?"

"No. This is something he has to do for himself."

"Yes. We can help him!" exclaimed Belle. "We'll go in and try and save him!" She was determined.

"Yes," said Betsy. "We can all go in. Maybe we can find out who is trying to kill him. We can help. I know we can."

213

"It won't do any good," said Tom.

"It won't do any harm either," said Ginny.

The girls all started clamoring again. Tom was outnumbered. They had made up their minds they were going to try to save Bolt and he could talk till he was blue in the face and he wouldn't change their minds.

"All right, all right," he said. "If you're so determined, we'll all go. I'm not going to let you ladies go in there by yourselves."

They hooted with delight. Belle ran to the bedroom, gathered up the spare weapons. She came back to the livingroom, doled them out like Friday paychecks.

"Just in case," she said.

****

Bolt had a lot of thinking to do on his way to town.

Too many lives had already been lost over this struggle for land. One more would die before it was over.

He hoped it wouldn't be him.

He wondered why most men couldn't allow a woman to find her own niche in this world, why they couldn't stand to see a woman succeed in a profession that was usually done by a man. It didn't seem fair that women were assigned their lot in life at the moment of birth, just because they happened to be born female.

He thought about the girls who worked for him at his two whorehouses. The glitter gals. True, they had chosen their profession, maybe not by choice, but it

214

was because the men expected it of them. Those girls had little chance to quit the business and do something on their own. Unless they got lucky and found someone who would marry them. Or until they got too old.

Bolt thought about his father who preached to his congregation, but who really didn't know the truth. The whores knew more truth about life than his father would ever know. He thought about his brother, Michael, who lived a lie for six years by blaming Bolt for the child that Michael had fathered.

He thought about his mother, whom he never knew, wondered what she would have been like.

He wondered about the man who was waiting for him in town this very minute. What was he like? Did he have a family?

This was the toughest kind of kill. Not knowing who your stalker was. It was frustrating. It was eerie. It was like facing someone blindfolded.

****

At the edge of town, Bolt pulled up on the reins. Holding onto the saddlehorn, he threw his leg over, stepped down out of the stirrup. He walked the horse over to a tall tree, looped the reins around a branch, tied it securely. He slapped the horse on the rump.

"Good boy," he said. "You wait right here for me. I hope I'll be back."

He slipped his pistol out of its holster, spun the cylinder, counted the bullets. Six. He slid it back in the holster.

He took a deep breath.

He was ready.

He walked to Main Street, strode down its middle.

Without any hesitation, he began the long walk. The town was only four blocks long, but it seemed a mile. He walked up the entire length of the main street of Black Mesa. Slow, measured steps.

His shooting hand hovered above his holster.

He was being watched, he knew. Not only by the one man, but by others in the small town. Curious people.

He walked up the street only once.

So anyone looking for him could see him plain.

When he reached the other end of the street, he turned around slowly, started back down the street.

The crowd had started to form. Men poured out of saloons, stores, businesses. Women peered out the smudgy windows.

People gathered in clusters to stare.

To watch the man who walked down the middle of the road.

Bolt saw the man who was waiting for him.

On the steps of the Pawnee Saloon.

He was leaning against a post.

Waiting.

Bolt now knew who the man was. He had seen him before. A long time ago.

"Is it you?" Bolt called out.

The man stepped away from the post. He walked to the middle of the street. To face Bolt.

"Yair, Bolt. 'Bout time. I shoulda taken you out back in Abilene. Trouble is, I don't work for free."

The two men were fifty feet apart. Getting closer with each step.

The man's hand hovered above his pistol.

Bolt's did the same.

"Horner paying you?"

"I don't ask where the money comes from."

"Maybe you should, Kendrick."

Kendrick went into a crouch. Twenty feet away.

He was fast.

Very fast.

Bolt was a shade faster.

Two shots rang out in the still air.

A second apart.

It was long enough for Bolt to duck.

Bolt knocked him down with a single shot.

Kendrick took the bullet in the heart. The impact knocked him backwards. He staggered. Two steps. Then collapsed to the ground, a silent curse on his lips. He was dead when he hit the ground. A pool of blood began to form beneath his body.

Bolt slipped his pistol back in its holster, turned away. He touched his cheek where a hairline of blood leaked from his flesh.

The curious crowd began to move around, came close to get a better look at the dead man. And the man who killed him. It would be a long time before they'd see another shoot-out that could match this one.

It was close.

Kendrick's bullet had just grazed Bolt's cheek.

That's how close it was.

****

Bolt froze where he was.

He saw the man moving in on him.

Johnny Von. Von's hand was extended as he pushed his way through the crowd. He lunged at Bolt.

Bolt couldn't believe it. He thought it was all over. It had to be over. The killings had to end.

Horner was there too. Coming up behind Von.

Bolt's hand flew to his holster.

He didn't have time to draw.

Von was right there before Bolt could think.

Von shoved his hand at Bolt, grabbed Bolt's hand.

"I just wanted to shake your hand," said Johnny. "I like your style."

Bolt breathed a sigh of relief, shook his head. Bolt thought back a few days, to the time he and Von had played poker. It was an honest game, on both sides. Von could have killed him there, when Bolt won the hands. But he hadn't. There had been big bounty money at stake, but Von took the loss like a man.

"I like your style, too," said Bolt.

Horner shoved his way past the onlookers, glared at Bolt. He looked down at the dead man.

"I'm leaving town," Horner said. "But we'll meet again some day."

"Pray that you don't, Horner."

Horner turned and walked away, a defeated man. He looked a hundred years old.

Bolt's smile was faint.

CHAPTER TWENTY-ONE

Tom and the three girls ran over from the other side of the street. They had arrived just in time to witness the shooting.

Betsy gasped when she saw her father's body on the ground, his chest stained with gore. The blood turned her stomach.

"Oh, no. Father, no."

"I'm sorry, Betsy," said Bolt.

"Is he . . . is he dead?"

"Yes, he's gone. Did you know, Betsy? About your father?"

"I never knew," she cried. "I suspected, but I never knew."

"What are you going to do now? Are you still going to leave town?"

"Yes. I can't stay here. I won't ever go back to Major. No matter what else happens to me, I never want to see that man again. He's the one who caused my father's death."

"You're strong. You'll make it."

"First, I'll take my father's body back to St. Louis for burial. After that, who knows?"

"You can come to work for me anytime you want," Bolt offered. "But I think you'd be happier if you started teaching again. Someday you'll find the right man. A good man who will love you."

"Thanks, Bolt."

"What about us?" asked Ginny. "You got a job for Belle and me?"

"You can dance in my place, and sing. That's it."

"Nothing else, Bolt?"

"Nope. Nothing else. You won't need the job anyway. Horner's place is up for sale. Buy it. Marry a rich guy. You and Belle both."

"That's a good idea," said Belle.

"I've even lined up a new foreman for you."

"You have?"

Bolt reached behind him, grabbed Johnny Von's arm, dragged him up to face Belle.

"Have you two met?" Bolt asked.

Belle was surprised. She recognized Johnny as one of Horner's men.

"Belle, this is Johnny Von. He's a good man."

Belle took a closer look at Johnny. A new twinkle came to her eye. Johnny was not unattractive. Maybe, just maybe, things would work out.

"What about you, Bolt?" said Ginny, a sadness in her voice. "What are you going to do?"

"I'm leaving town."

"When?"

"Today. As soon as I can gather up my things. I'll be gone before sundown. I'll leave Tom here to handle the loose ends. Think he's got some unfinished business of his own anyway."

"Sure do," smiled Tom. "I'll be happy to stay."

"Do you have to leave so soon, Bolt?" asked Belle.

"I can't figure you women out. First you beg me to leave town, practically chase me out with a broom stick. Now you're begging me to stay. I guess I'll never understand you."

Their laughter relieved the tension.

The crowd started to break up as people drifted away.

Betsy stood by her father's body until the undertaker came with a buckboard and carted him away.

Tom headed for the Roosters Nest.

Betsy walked away with Johnny Von, her arm looped through his.

Ginny held back, waiting to say goodbye to Bolt.

"I wish I could go with you," she said when they were alone.

"I do too. But it wouldn't work."

"I know." She paused, saw the thin line of blood on his cheek. "You're hurt."

"Just a scratch," he said.

"Bolt, do you remember what you told me the other day? After we made love? When I told you I wanted to spend a whole night with you?"

"I remember. I said I owed you one."

"You said it was a promise."

He looked down at her and smiled.

"I always keep my promise."

She took his hand, squeezed it.

"Can you stay the night?" she asked.

"I'll stay. And I'll promise you something else."

"What's that?"

"There won't be any interruptions. Everyone else will think I'm long gone."

She laughed, her voice a musical tinkle.

****

Bolt rose early the next morning. Ginny was still asleep in the hotel bed. Her dark hair fanned out around her face.

Bolt leaned down and kissed her softly on the forehead. He wouldn't wake her up. It was better that way.

He hated goodbyes.

The morning sky was turning pale cream when he mounted his horse.

It would be a good day to travel.

It wasn't until he was out of town that he began missing Ginny.

But, it was not in him to settle down.

Not yet.

Life was just too damned good his way.

WORLD WAR II—
FROM THE GERMAN POINT OF VIEW